OTHER BOOKS AND AUDIO BOOKS
BY JEFFREY S. SAVAGE:

Cutting Edge

Into the Fire

HOUSE OF
SECRETS

HOUSE OF SECRETS

a Shandra
Covington
mystery

JEFFREY S. SAVAGE

Covenant Communications, Inc.

Covenant®

Cover design by Jessica A. Warner © 2005 by Covenant Communications, Inc.
Cover image by Patrick Koslo © Brand X Pictures/Getty Images, Inc.

Published by Covenant Communications, Inc.
American Fork, Utah

Printed in Canada
First Printing: October 2005

11 10 09 08 07 06 05   10 9 8 7 6 5 4 3 2 1

ISBN 1-59811-006-3

In loving memory of the grandmothers:

Elsie Davis Apsley	13 Feb 1907 – 31 Oct 1996
Barbara Paine Martin	18 Oct 1916 – 19 Sept 2004
Helen Bertram Mauritz	17 Apr 1913 – 4 Mar 1972
Martha Harris Sheppard	17 Oct 1915 – 7 Sept 1998

ACKNOWLEDGMENTS

Special thanks to all of the following for their great input. Any mistakes happened because I didn't listen closely enough.

The Spanish Fork and Payson Police Departments for their insights on police procedure. Shane Youd for all things farming related. Steven Blackhurst, who pulled the original shoe-tying trick—on himself. My parents, brothers, and sisters for their great input. The ladies of Wednesday night (you know who you are), for excellent critiques. Kirk Shaw, Peter Jasinski, and the rest of the Covenant staff for professional advice and direction. (Shauna Humphreys, you will be missed.) William Sheehy, who lit the fire more than twenty years ago. It hasn't gone out. To my great children for sacrificing dad time so I could get this out. And as always to my first and last reader, the person who makes everything else worthwhile, my wife, Jennifer. You're the best.

CHAPTER ONE

They say the human subconscious is capable of picking up hidden danger signals long before the conscious mind is aware that anything's wrong. The senses tingle. The small hairs on the back of the neck stand. Adrenaline races through the body. It's supposed to be a holdover from the times when having a bad day meant ending up inside a saber tooth's belly.

Well, maybe I'm just not in touch with my inner cavewoman. Or maybe my receiver was on the fritz that day. Whatever the case, I don't remember feeling any sense of peril, no premonitions of impending doom, as I reached the top of the rise revealing the house on the hillside.

My name is Shandra Covington. I'm a reporter for the *Deseret Morning News,* Utah's second largest daily paper. Sound glamorous? Try writing six hundred words on the umpteenth charity fund-raiser you've attended that month while Chad Nettle, my editor, breathes fire down your neck at one in the morning. Throw in a bimonthly check that lasts almost exactly three days short of the next payday, and you've pretty much summed up my life.

If that still sounds glamorous, you've got to get out more.

To the best of my recollection, as I pulled my little MGB off the road as far up the overgrown drive as I dared, my subconscious and conscious minds were both pretty tied up demanding to know why I hadn't eaten anything since breakfast. They were also wondering where I could find a bacon-double-cheeseburger, heavy on the pickles and onions, with steak fries and one of those chocolate shakes you have to eat with a spoon.

I know that sounds more like a trucker's meal than the afternoon repast of a five-one blonde who still has to buy most of her clothes in the *girls'* section. What can I say? I have a fast metabolism.

The other women at work give me a lot of flak about my appetite. *How can you eat like that? It's unfair,* and *I'm so jealous.* But none of them have to ask the clerk at Mervyn's, "Do you have these jeans *without* Winnie the Pooh on the pocket?"

Trying to ignore the gurgling sounds coming from my stomach, I took off the baseball cap that keeps me from turning into a puffball when I drive with the top down, and shook out my hair.

"Well, Royce, we're here," I said, taking my camera from the passenger's seat. My car's name is Royce, as in Rolls Royce. If I can dream of winning a Pulitzer Prize one day, why can't he have dreams of his own? He ticked back at me contentedly.

When I'd left Salt Lake, it had been a sweltering ninety-eight degrees—a typical July day. But in the mountains of northeastern Utah, it was at least fifteen degrees cooler. Waist-high grass—still green and lush up here—pressed against the car door as I pushed it open and got out.

Tucking my hands into the back pockets of my jeans, I surveyed the hybrid structure, half log cabin, half two-story Victorian, and the woods beyond it. It was the first time I'd seen Gam's house in over twenty years.

The place looked smaller, more ordinary than my childhood memories of it. I took in the sagging front porch. Wild lilacs were pushing up through several of its splintery boards. The white paint and green trim were peeling, and although none of the windows were broken (surprising after all this time), they were coated with thick layers of grime. Around the side, the rusty old propane tank looked like the world's biggest and dirtiest cold capsule.

Still, despite the disrepair, some of the old magic remained. Maybe it was the way the thick groves of aspen and pine crowded close, the crystal blue waters of Echo Lake just visible through their spread branches.

As a little girl, I'd sit beneath those trees listening to my grandmother tell me about Hansel and Gretel or Sleeping Beauty. After the stories, as we walked down to the lake, I'd scatter bits of my tuna sandwich behind me, imagining that somewhere in those woods was an enticing little gingerbread house.

Shaking my head—as if I could physically clear out the memories—I reminded myself that I was here to sell the house Gam had left to my brother and me. Reliving childhood memories couldn't bring my grandmother back. And if she *had* been there, she would undoubtedly have scolded me for not focusing on the present. Gam was big on leaving the past in the past.

I checked my watch. It was not quite two. If I was quick, I could snap a few pictures of the house to use in the listing, sign the real estate agreement, and get something to fill my stomach before heading back to the city. Lifting the Nikon that hung from a strap around my neck, I adjusted the aperture for the bright sunlight and grimaced at what I saw. This was going to require some seriously creative photography, preferably shot from a great distance with lots trees filling the frame.

The still of the afternoon was broken by the snuffle, rattle, and cough of a laboring engine. I turned in time to see an ancient-looking pickup come trundling up the road. Abruptly the driver swung the steering wheel hard to the right and brought the truck to a shuddering stop amid a cloud of thick, blue exhaust.

Lowering my camera, I read the filthy sign on the passenger door: PETE'S CONCRETE AND MASONRY. The phone number was buried beneath a heavy layer of dirt. I tried to make out the driver's features through the clouded windshield. He did the same with me. Leaning across the seat, he rolled down the window. As the glass slowly lowered it made a high-pitched squeal like a fork scraping china.

"You lost, missie?" The brown, lined face—Pete's, I presumed—stared out at me from under the bill of an old green baseball cap. Gleaming white teeth that could only be dentures smiled behind leathery lips.

"I'm fine," I called, giving a half wave.

The blue eyes narrowed suspiciously, the smile dimming a little.

"This is my grandmother's house," I explained. "She passed away recently."

Pete blinked, lifting his cap a notch. He looked me up and down. "Thought you looked familiar. Elsie was purty as a picture." He picked at something between his teeth with the edge of his thumbnail and nodded slowly. "You're the spitting image of her."

"Um, thanks." I kicked at the back tire of my car, feeling the blood rush to my face and hating it.

I've never been one to accept compliments easily. I think it comes from growing up as a tomboy. Until I was twelve or so, if anyone dared to call me pretty, I'd split their lip. After that, the boys must have gotten the idea, because no one ever called me pretty in high school. They never asked me out either. Their loss.

"Say she's dead?" His lips puckered, deep grooves creasing his forehead.

"A week ago Thursday." I expected that once I told him who I was, he'd be back on his way. But he showed no signs of leaving and kept watching me from under the brim of his cap.

Uncomfortable under his stare, I pointed back toward the house. "I just came to snap a few pictures, take a walk through the place. My brother and I are putting the house up for sale."

A cloud crossed Pete's face, as though I'd suggested selling my grandmother instead of just her house.

"No one's used the place in more than twenty years," I said, feeling a little defensive. "To tell you the truth, I didn't even know Gam still owned it until I saw her will. She never talked about it."

Something in my words had an immediate impact on the old man, or maybe it was just the dawning realization of Gam's death. His mouth clamped down, like a desert tortoise pulling back into its shell. "No, don't imagine she would," he finally said, his voice rusty.

"Why do you say that?" I asked. But my question was drowned out by a shriek of clashing metal, as Pete dropped back into his seat and forced the pickup into first gear.

If he'd heard me, he didn't bother to answer. The old truck began to ease forward as Pete stared at Gam's house with an unreadable expression.

"Wouldn't stick around here, if I was you." His words were so soft I almost couldn't make them out beneath the labored rattle and clang of the engine. I stepped toward the side of the truck, but he waved me away with a callused hand.

"No," he said, shaking his head as if I'd contradicted him. "Wouldn't stick around here at all. Might not be safe."

With that, he pulled back onto the road and disappeared behind a blue plume of smoke.

What was that all about? While I might not be a guy magnet, I'd never actively scared men away.

With the possible exception of the time I fell into a basement full of raw sewage while covering a story for my first paper, the *Twin Forks Gazette*. But even then, I could blame my blind date's hasty retreat on the fact that he arrived at my apartment a full fifteen minutes early—getting there just as I shambled up the walk like the Creature from the Black Lagoon. Conjure up the worst smells you can think of—rotten eggs, dirty diapers, the Great Salt Lake on a hot summer day, its shore covered with dead brine shrimp—and multiply them by a hundred. That will give you some idea of how bad I stunk.

His abrupt departure was at least understandable—if slightly unfair. Pete's actions were just strange. As I stood at the edge of the road, the roar of the truck engine fading away to the silence that had preceded the old man's appearance, I replayed our conversation in my mind.

What had he said just before he drove off—something about not being safe? Had he been threatening me? I didn't think so. He didn't seem the type (unless he was planning on bricking me inside a wine cellar like the guy in that Poe story). But he had certainly been worked up.

With an uneasy glance at the warped boards, I tentatively climbed the steps to the front porch. Prepared to turn tail at the first sign of collapsing timbers, I approached the door. Despite their weathered appearance, the boards seemed stable enough beneath my feet.

I placed a hand on the doorknob, and all at once a disturbing thought occurred to me. What if there was someone inside the house? It was Gam's, but for all intents and purposes she had abandoned it years ago. What if someone had taken up residence in the meantime? A transient, a deadbeat . . . or something worse.

Snatching my hand away from the knob, I checked for signs that anyone else had been there. Nothing obvious caught my eye—no rusty beer cans, old newspapers, or trampled grass. Still, I couldn't help feeling as though someone were watching me from inside the darkened windows. The encroaching trees that had seemed enchanting before, now felt menacing, their branches grasping hands stretching toward me.

I should have turned and left. Would have, if not for my contrary nature. Ever since I was little, my stubborn streak has gotten me into trouble. Steve Jr., my older brother by two years, always swore that if someone wanted to kill me when we were kids all they had to do was tell me not to jump off a cliff.

I've mellowed a little over time, at least I'd like to think I have, but the idea of anyone running me out of my grandmother's house hit a nerve. Before I could change my mind, I grabbed the knob, shoved the door open—and gasped.

CHAPTER TWO

I stood in the bright sunlight, my eyes gradually adjusting to the dark interior. But my mind refused to adjust to what I was seeing. On the drive up, I'd just assumed my grandmother's house would be empty. After all, it had been more than two decades since Gam left her home and moved in with us, shortly after my father abandoned our family.

Secretly I might have hoped to run across some kind of memento—perhaps an old letter or a discarded photograph. But any of her belongings would be long gone. After all, who moved without taking their things?

And yet, staring into the open doorway, I realized that was exactly what Gam had done.

The loveseat with the twining rose pattern, the afghan hanging over its back, the brass lamp that always reminded me of a big one-legged flamingo, the painting of a lone lighthouse jutting out into the sea—everything was there, just as I remembered it, only covered with layer upon layer of dust.

It was like looking into one of those haunted houses they set up for Halloween. Spiderwebs had been built, fallen apart, and been rebuilt so many times that the entire room seemed to be slightly in motion. From every surface, gauzy gray fingers swayed in the breeze I'd created by opening the door.

Heart pounding, fingers trembling, I entered the room. A sour odor assaulted my nostrils. Something scrabbled across the floor. I was halfway out the door before realizing what it was.

Over the years, creatures had moved into the house. *Mice,* I thought, trying not to imagine anything bigger. The air was heavy with the ammonia-like stink of animal droppings that reminded me of the primate house at the zoo.

I waited for the smell to clear out a little, then stepped forward into the gloom, trying to comprehend what I was seeing.

On the coffee table to my left lay a paperback book, its dust-coated pages spread on the table like the wings of some great gray moth. I picked it up and wiped the cover on the leg of my jeans. Several of the pages fell from their binding, but the title was easily readable. *Call of the Wild,* by Jack London. I'd read it in high school.

Through the kitchen doorway, I could see a saucepan on the counter, and beside it, what looked like an old soup can. The label had long since disintegrated, but I knew that it would be Campbell's Tomato—Gam's favorite.

What was going on here? My grandmother wasn't fastidious, but she was neat. She never left the house without at least straightening up a little. This didn't look like the house of someone who planned to move. But why?

Until that moment, I'd never really given any thought to why my grandmother left her house. I was just a kid when she moved in with us, still trying to cope with the fact that my dad had deserted our family six months earlier, in pretty much the same fashion Grandpa left Gam years before. If pressed for a reason, I guess I would have said that my mommy needed her mommy. I was just happy to have her there.

Had I ever considered what had become of Gam's possessions? Her furniture, her porcelain figurines, the intricate
jigsaw puzzles she was always putting together? If so, I
couldn't remember.

Turning, I could clearly see my footprints in the thick
dust that covered the hardwood floor. I was standing in the
half of the house that had originally been a two-room
cabin—built by my great-grandfather James Sullivan in the
1920s. I could remember sliding across the polished pine
boards in my stocking feet as a child. Gam had taken great
pride in keeping the floor highly waxed and polished so that
it gleamed a mellow gold in the afternoon sun.

Now, kneeling to brush away more of the dust, I could
see that part of the floor's surface had been marred by a dark
stain. Maybe the tomato soup she'd been cooking. And yet,
despite the hot mustiness of the house, I felt tiny bumps
breaking out across my arms and shoulders. There was
another splotch by the front doorway, and a larger spot a
little farther in.

At the foot of the stairs—the dividing line between the
old cabin and the new wing that Great-grandfather Sullivan
had added on twenty years later—I noticed more of the
stains, as though someone had carried a paintbrush up the
stairs, carelessly dripping and spilling as they walked. I
reached down to touch the dark substance that had soaked
into the wood, before pulling my hand back uneasily.

Above me, the stairwell was a maze of cobwebs. Fending
the hanging strands off with one arm—trying to keep them
from touching my face—I climbed the steps one at a time.
Hung along the wall, in an ascending line, was a row of
picture frames. I rubbed at the glass-covered portraits, my

touch revealing faces peering out at me through the dust. Some I recognized, many more I didn't.

At one I stopped. It was a black-and-white of my grandmother, taken in front of her house. She looked to be in her mid-forties—before I was born, but some years after Grandpa had left her.

I studied her eyes, searching for traces of sadness—of loneliness. If they were there, I couldn't find them. To me she looked firm, resolute. I wished that I'd had this portrait to use for her obituary. Gam didn't like having her picture taken, and the only one I'd been able to find as I rushed about making funeral arrangements was a wedding photo of her and Grandpa that I'd located in my mother's album.

The next picture was of my mother and father. They couldn't have been any older than their early twenties. An odd lump filled my throat as I lifted the frame from the wall and cleared the glass surface with the palm of my hand. They looked so young. It was strange to see them cheerful.

Three years after Gam came to live with us—just before my tenth birthday—my mother was killed in a car accident, leaving Gam to raise us single-handedly. The memories I have of my mother, and the few of my father, are not generally happy ones. I'd assumed that the worry lines bracketing Mom's eyes and mouth had always been there. That my father had always been an angry and taciturn man. But these were the faces of a carefree couple, very much in love by the looks of it. When had all that changed?

Brushing off the picture frame, I saw that it was sterling silver, raising another question. Why hadn't anyone looted the place after all these years? Echo Lake was a small town. Most people probably didn't even bother to lock their doors at night. But still, after twenty plus years, wouldn't a curious kid or two have broken in—at least to explore? Although Gam wasn't wealthy, there were definitely things of value here. And the only signs of entry I could see were the occasional rodent tracks.

I finished climbing the stairs and stopped outside a closed door. Gam's bedroom. When I came to visit, I'd slept in the guest room across the hall. But if I started to feel scared or lonely, I could creep through this door, knowing that Gam would let me snuggle with her under the thick goose-down quilt.

Placing my left hand on the dark wood, I paused. Though Gam had been dead for almost two weeks, I felt like an intruder here.

Almost of its own volition, my hand pushed the door. Years of disuse had left the hinges dry and rusted. They cried out softly as I pressed them into use. The first thing I noticed was the smell. Apparently the mice hadn't made it into this room. Even after all the years, the faint perfume of violets—Gam's favorite scent—was clearly discernible.

There was another smell too. Something that made me think of the paperback book downstairs. It was like old newspapers, weathered by time until they would crumble at the first touch. The second odor, slipping stealthily from beneath Gam's fragrance, made me uneasy.

Although I knew there was no one else in the house with me, I couldn't shake the feeling that I wasn't alone. It was as if the memories here had been locked up for so long that they'd taken on a weight and substance of their own.

I scanned the room, noting nothing out of the ordinary. The bed was made with Gam's usual neatness, although it too was covered with a dark gray coat of dust and cobwebs. As I crossed to the foot of the bed, a flash of movement caught my eye. Turning, I stared into a pair of wide, shocked eyes.

A squeak of fear escaped my throat before I realized the eyes I was staring into were my own. It was just a mirror, my reflection dim beneath its murky surface. Putting a hand to my chest, I tried to calm my heart's trip-hammer pounding.

I grimaced and stuck out my tongue. I meant it as a way to banish my fright, to prove that there really was no boogeyman in here. But the face floating up from the depths of the dark glass looked so unlike my own that I immediately pulled back my tongue and dropped my eyes.

On the dresser next to the mirror, I saw something that brought back a flood of emotion. It was a wooden box, about eight inches wide by six inches deep. I recognized it instantly as Gam's music box. I had one at home just like it. It had belonged to my mother, but it hadn't worked for years.

I turned the box over and examined the silver handle on the bottom. Afraid that it would be frozen, I carefully began to twist. The handle moved easily beneath my fingers, and I could hear the click, click, click of a motor inside as I wound the spring.

When I opened the lid, a tiny couple sprang to life, accompanied by the tinny melody that had fascinated me as a girl. Watching the man in his black tux and the woman in her pink formal spin across the mirrored surface of the music box, I remembered how I'd dreamt of being a dancer. I guess most girls think about that at some point in their lives. My dreams lasted right up until I realized I had all the rhythm of a water buffalo.

"Yeah, well, being a reporter beats the snot out of being a dancer anyway," I said, with only a trace of sour grapes.

Closing the music box and setting it back on the dresser, I noticed something reflected in the mirror. Lying on the floor, half in and half out of the closet, it looked like a length of driftwood.

Approaching it, I could see that the piece of wood was nearly six feet long and had been wrapped in some kind of cloth. Why would Gam have hauled a log up into her room? I reached down and turned it over. It was surprisingly light and moved easily beneath my hand.

"What—" I began, before my mind grasped what my eyes were seeing. The muscles in my jaw froze. My fingers seemed unable to release their grip. Once again a cry of fear began to tear itself from my throat. Only this time there would be no stopping it. The log I was holding—what had looked like an old piece of driftwood—was the mummified remains of a human body.

CHAPTER THREE

I found myself somehow back at my car, hands propped on the hood to support my wobbly knees. My head was spinning. *I touched it. I actually had my hands on it.* The thought roared over and over in my head, setting my stomach roiling.

As a journalist, I'd seen my share of dead bodies—many in worse condition than the one in the house. But that was business. This had been so unexpected. So *personal.*

I wiped my hands fiercely up and down the legs of my jeans—trying not to remember how the corpse's sunken eyes had stared up at me, his wrinkled skin weathered to the dark, hard consistency of those dried apple dolls.

"Stop it." My words came out in a voice I barely recognized, and I bit down on the inside of my cheeks, trying to get myself under control. Taking slow, deep breaths, I held my hands out in front of me, waiting for them to stop shaking.

I assessed the situation. I wasn't in any imminent danger. The body in the house had been dead for a long, long time. Whatever happened to it had happened years before. Still my mind kept running into the idea—just like a pinball runs into a bumper and gets shot away—that there was actually a corpse in my grandmother's house. Who was it? How did it get there? Had Gam known about it? Surely not, but . . .

Opening the car door, I slipped behind the wheel. The familiarity of my car's leather interior around me, and the knowledge that I could be gone in a flash at the first sign of anything untoward, eased my mind considerably. My keys were still hanging from the ignition. I turned them, bringing the engine to life.

I hazarded a glance at the front porch, half-convinced that I would see a dark figure shambling out of the doorway, or a face peering from one of the windows. Nothing. Still, any magic Gam's house held for me was long gone.

You have to notify the authorities. It was the first clear thought I'd come up with, and I clung to it like a life raft. Okay, right. Contact the authorities. I could do that. I fished my cell phone from the handbag on the passenger's seat.

9-1-1. I pressed the buttons that suddenly felt far too small for my trembling fingers and put the phone to my ear.

Silence. Why wasn't the call going through? I started to dial again before belatedly realizing there was no service out here.

As the shock of what I'd seen began to wear off, rational thought slowly made its way back into my brain. There was a sheriff's office in town. I would drive down to Main Street— the direction Pete had been coming from—and would report what I'd found. They would know what to do.

Pressing in the clutch, I shifted the leather-covered handle of the stick shift into reverse and began to back up. Halfway onto the road, the meaning of what I'd seen dawned on me. My foot left the gas pedal. The transmission cried out in protest, and the car jerked backward before the engine died.

The body. The house. Gam's silence about it. The pieces suddenly meshed, and a soft moan escaped my lips. Had my grandmother killed someone?

CHAPTER FOUR

"What can I get you, hon?" The woman behind the counter of Big Mike's reminded me of an older version of my mother—what she might look like if she were still alive. Her face was longer, her nose sharper, but she had the same stern gray eyes, the same spray of wrinkles that spoke of endurance through hard times.

I was sitting in Big Mike's, a diner toward the end of Echo Lake's main drag. Big Mike had apparently made a half-hearted attempt at a '50s motif. The chairs and stools were all upholstered in sparkly red vinyl, the tables topped with white Formica.

Big Mike's clientele appeared to consist almost exclusively of locals, based on the preponderance of pickups in the parking lot and the number of diners dressed in denim and work boots. I imagined that the tourists favored the more expensive restaurants uptown or left Echo Lake altogether to eat out. I noticed people glancing in my direction—wondering, I'm sure, who I was—but I didn't mind. I'll take quality and quantity of food over ambiance every time.

Holding the menu in hands I'd scrubbed red in the restaurant bathroom, I placed my order. "I'll have a double stack of hotcakes with ham, bacon, and hash browns, English muffins, and a large orange juice."

I'll eat anything in a pinch, but breakfast is, and always will be, my comfort food. Just the smell of hot maple syrup makes me want to snug into a pair of footie pajamas and curl up next to a fire. Right now I needed comfort.

The waitress scribbled on a pink pad, her eyes registering only slight surprise at the quantity of my order. Tucking the pad back into her pocket, she paused, her eyes giving me a once-over.

"Do I know you, hon?" she asked, tapping a stubby pencil against her lower lip.

All at once I wondered if I should have gone up to one of the touristy places after all. Right now the last thing I wanted was anyone asking me about Gam. I shook my head. "I don't think so."

"Gosh, I coulda sworn . . ." She turned back to the kitchen and tucked my order slip onto a little metal wheel, but every so often I caught her glancing back in my direction.

Fiddling with my napkin, I avoided her stares. What was I feeling guilty about anyway? It wasn't like I had anything to do with the body. And I fully intended to go straight to the sheriff's office . . . just as soon as I worked a few things out. As I listened to the clattering of utensils and inhaled the aromas of the kitchen, I tried to come up with a plausible explanation for what I'd found.

The first thing I had to do was take a step back and separate my assumptions from the facts. I never go anywhere without my little brown leather backpack. It's my compromise between purses, which I can't stand, and trying to fit everything in my pockets, which I dislike even worse. I took out a pen and notepad, and began to make a list, letting my reporter-self take over.

Beside the number one I wrote *Body*. Was I sure I had seen a body? Yes, absolutely. Was I sure it was dead? If it wasn't, it was going to have some serious rehydration issues when it woke up. Okay, so the dead body in Gam's bedroom was a fact.

Next I wrote *Who?* Based on the hair and the height, I assumed it was a man. But I really didn't want to dwell any further on the face I'd seen. Besides, I hadn't been to Echo Lake since I was about six. What where the chances that I'd know anyone up here? I left the who question blank for the time being.

Around me, customers came and went, accompanied by the usual restaurant noises—the clatter of plates and silverware, the ca-ching of the register, the sound of eating and greeting. But none of them fazed me. When I was working on a story I could be very single minded.

Cause of death came next. Discovering the body unexpectedly, my first assumption was that it had been killed. But I really didn't know that at all. Couldn't it have been a squatter who keeled over from a heart attack? *A squatter who reads Jack London and eats tomato soup,* an annoying little voice in my head piped up. *And since when do heart-attack victims bleed across the room and up the stairs?*

Okay, so it wasn't a heart attack. That didn't automatically make it a murder either. The guy could have slipped and hit his head. He wandered upstairs, collapsed, and died. The very fact that no one had come looking for him could support the squatter theory.

But how did I explain Gam's things or the fact that to the best of my knowledge she'd never returned to her house or even mentioned it? And while I was considering the unexplainable, how about clearing up the mystery of how a dead body in an abandoned house could go unnoticed long enough for the body to desiccate?

"Get you anything else, hon?" The waitress brought my food, and for the next few minutes, any further thought was lost in the depths of melted butter, hot syrup, and crisp bacon.

"Hungry, are you?" The question came from a man sitting two stools over.

"No," I snipped without bothering to look over. "When I'm hungry I get the T-bone steak, too."

I hate it when people comment about how much I eat, especially strangers. These people would never dream of telling someone, "You have a really bony behind," or, "Do you know your cologne is strong enough to ignite an open flame?" But somehow they find it perfectly acceptable to comment on other people's dietary habits.

Apparently he didn't catch the tone of my voice though, because he broke into a startled laugh. Even in my agitated state, I couldn't help but notice how nice his laugh was—not too loud or too nasal. It sounded full and unforced, like it originated deep inside.

"I'll keep my dinner away from you," he said.

I glanced briefly in his direction. He had an open face, handsome in a down-home sort of way. A nice smile, too, teeth white, but not Donny Osmond perfect.

"Look," I said, trying to adopt a more conciliatory tone. "I don't mean to be rude, but I've got a lot on my mind right now." That was the understatement of the century.

I expected him to try at least one come-on line. Not that I'm any prize, but country boys always seem to think they're hot stuff, and this one looked like he probably did pretty well with the ladies.

Instead he sketched a quick salute with his first two fingers. "Nuff said." And turned back to his dinner.

I watched him dig into his mashed potatoes without another glance in my direction. That had been too easy, and I found myself wishing that he'd put up at least a token fight. Feeling as if I'd somehow been insulted, I finished eating the rest of my food.

With my stomach quieted for the time being, my thoughts returned to the body. I had to decide what to do about it, and I knew that I was putting it off. Not that I had a lot of choice in the matter. It wasn't like I could just leave it there. Imagine the real estate listing: Fully furnished 3 br, 1 1/2 bath, cozy kitchen, lake view, dead body in upstairs closet.

But what if Gam had known about the body? What if that's why she left? I racked my brain for any conversation we might have had about why she'd left her house. The only thing I could come up with was a vague sense of uneasiness on her part when the subject came up once, and a feeling that maybe, years ago, she'd promised to tell me about it when I was older.

If she'd kept it a secret all these years, she must have had her reasons. By going to the police I'd be breaking a confidence of the woman who became a second mother to my brother and me.

But once again, it wasn't like I had a lot of options. I could notify the authorities or pretend that I'd never seen the body and let someone else discover it, or . . . what? Get rid of the body? It sounded like one of those *CSI* episodes. "Gil, according to our spectrograph analysis, it was the woman's granddaughter. She disposed of the body to avoid casting suspicion on her grandmother."

Like I'd even have the first clue about how to hide a dead body. The best I could come up with was a vague picture of me digging a hole in the middle of the woods on a moonless night, or rowing out to the middle of Echo Lake with a bunch of weights attached to a chain.

I considered calling Bobby Richter. My best friend since first grade, he's a cop in the Salt Lake P.D. He'd do almost anything for me, and I'd gotten him out of more than one bind. If I asked him to come up, he'd be there in a heartbeat—after complaining for ten or fifteen minutes about how I was putting him out.

But I knew what he'd say. He'd bawl me out for even waiting this long to go to the sheriff. I could practically hear his voice, high-pitched and overflowing with moral indignation. "Do you have any idea how many laws you're breaking by not reporting something like this?"

The thought of Bobby throwing a conniption made me smile. He's a lot of fun when he gets riled up. I knew what I had to do though. And I didn't need Bobby to tell me. I'd sleep on it just to be sure. But first thing in the morning I'd go see the sheriff.

Against my will, the image of the face I'd seen floated back to the top of my mind. It had been almost unrecognizable as human—skin dry and shriveled like beef jerky, eyes like raisins. Still, something about it had seemed almost familiar. I shouldn't have been able to tell anything of its features. Couldn't have. And yet . . .

With a nagging certainty I realized what my mind already knew. The food in my stomach churned, and I put a hand to my mouth. I was pretty sure that I'd seen the features on that face before. My mother's firm jaw line, my brother's prominent brow, my own high cheekbones.

As much as it terrified me, I thought the face had been my grandfather's.

CHAPTER FIVE

Standing outside the sheriff's office, I took a deep breath, once again telling myself I was doing the right thing. After hours of tossing and turning on a lumpy mattress in a cheap motel, I hadn't come up with a better plan.

Now, with the sun barely glinting over the mountains to the east, I swallowed hard and pushed my way through the door. "Eat a frog first thing in the morning and things can only get better," I whispered to myself, quoting one of Gam's favorite adages.

In this case the proverb ended up not being entirely accurate.

"Uh, oh. Hide the doughnuts!" a voice called out as I stepped into the lobby. It took me a moment to recognize the uniformed man sitting behind the desk. When I did, I could feel color rise to my face.

"You're the guy from the diner," I said lamely.

"Sorry," he said, looking anything but. "That was a mean thing to say."

"I guess I deserved it after last night." This wasn't going exactly the way I'd planned, and I wondered if I should come back later, maybe when he wasn't on duty.

He stood up from behind the desk, tall and rangy, and walked toward me. "Let's start again," he said with just a touch of rural Utah drawl. "I didn't get your name last time we met."

"Shandra Covington." I looked up to meet his eyes. That's another thing that bugs me about being short, always having to look up at people—though over the years I've gotten used to it—almost.

"Clay Weller." He shook hands like a returned missionary, his grip dry and a little too enthusiastic.

"You're the sheriff?" I asked.

"Nope. Sheriff Orr doesn't come on duty for another hour or so. I'm his deputy." He seemed nice enough, if perhaps a little wet behind the ears.

"Maybe I ought to come back in later," I said. I didn't want to have to repeat my story when the sheriff came in. On the other hand, I didn't know if I could wait an hour without losing my nerve completely.

"You could do that." Clay nodded. "Got plenty of doughnuts while you wait." He shot me one of those hangdog grins that I would have kicked him in the kneecap for if the doughnuts hadn't actually sounded pretty good.

He pointed me to a chair and slid over a box with RISE & SHINE BAKERY printed on the front. "They're tasty," he said, with no trace of a smile.

I wouldn't give him the satisfaction. Crossing my legs, I glanced around the office. Clay looked up from whatever he was typing on the computer. I specifically avoided looking at the doughnut box. He returned to his work.

What the heck. I guessed it wouldn't hurt just to lift the lid and take a peek. The next thing I knew, I had finished a jelly doughnut and was halfway through a chocolate-covered bar. I'm a slave to my appetite.

Clay watched me eat with a poorly hidden grin. At least he had the good sense not to make any comments.

"Thanks," I mumbled after I'd finished both of the pastries. I wiped my hands on a napkin, trying not to think about the bear claw that was still in the box.

"No problem," he said. He pulled the container across the desk and took the bear claw. I looked away.

"So is there anything I can help you with?" he asked, biting and chewing with agonizing satisfaction.

I shook my head, trying not to watch him eat.

"Did you get a ticket or something? There's no overnight parking allowed on Main." How long could a person chew one bite?

"No. It's nothing like that." I wished the sheriff would arrive. I'd come here to get everything off my chest, and now I was starting to have second thoughts.

"Been a string of car break-ins since summer. Couple of folks got their radios stolen." He took a second bite and smacked his lips.

"No one would want my car radio. It only plays AM, and even then it sounds like it's coming across one of those tin can phones."

He nodded, wiping his lips with a napkin, and set the bear claw on his desk. Wasn't he even going to finish it?

"One woman had her purse stolen right out of her shopping cart at the Sack'N'Save."

Suddenly I couldn't take it anymore. I stood, snatched up the rest of the bear claw, and downed it in one quick swallow. "It's not a robbery, and it's not a ticket, and no one took my purse!" I shouted, trying not to spray crumbs. "It's a *body*. I found a dead body!"

CHAPTER SIX

"I'm going to ask you to stay outside while we take a look around." Sheriff Orr was shorter than Clay, but what he lacked in height he made up for in girth. His face was doughy and slightly pink, as though he were recovering from a bad sunburn. He waved a pudgy hand toward me, and I stepped back to the edge of the porch. I was in no hurry to see the body again anyway.

The sheriff unsnapped his holster, and Clay did the same. It seemed a little melodramatic as far as I was concerned. After all, it wasn't like the murderer was going to be standing on the stairs, waiting to ambush them.

Sheriff Orr nodded at Clay to go first. Real brave. Clay glanced quickly in my direction and then pushed open the front door. They both tensed as if waiting for something to jump out at them.

It was all I could do to keep from shouting, "He's dead for crying out loud!"

"Looks like it's empty," the sheriff declared.

Well, duh.

Both men carried flashlights on their belts, and now they unclipped them to shine in the doorway. The morning sun was behind the house, doing little to illuminate the room.

Sheriff Orr started to step through the door, but Clay put a hand on his arm.

"Hang on." The sheriff stopped as Clay pointed to something on the floor. They both looked back in my direction.

"You said you were the only one who entered the house yesterday?" Sheriff Orr asked, glancing toward the door.

"Yes." I edged a little closer trying to see what they were looking at.

"And you didn't tell anyone else about what you saw?"

"No. Just you two." I moved even closer, and now I could see partway through the door. It was hard to make out much more than shapes in the dim interior, but from what I could see, nothing had changed since I'd been there last.

"I think you better wait in the car."

Sheriff Orr put out his arm to stop me from going any farther, but not before I'd managed to get close enough to see what had stopped them. On the floor, clearly illuminated by Clay's flashlight, were the footprints I'd made going into and out of the house. My footprints going in were spaced closely together while my footprints coming back out were spaced more widely apart, showing signs of skidding.

But now there was something new in the dust—something that hadn't been there the day before. Alongside the footprints I'd made were a second pair, much bigger—a man's footprints. They followed my prints across the room and up the staircase.

The bigger footprints led into the house. But there were none leading back out.

CHAPTER SEVEN

I sat crouched on the backseat of the police cruiser, expecting at any minute to hear gunshots or see a figure come hurtling through the front door of Gam's house. In the event of the former I'd lie low until the violence was over and then head in to cover the story.

And in the event of the latter, my legs were hanging out the side of the car only inches from the ground. If the person who came out the front door was not wearing a uniform, I was ready to hightail it into the woods.

Clay had tried to convince me that I'd be safer locked inside the car, but I'd heard plenty of horror stories where the police go into the house armed to the teeth, and the bad guy comes out carrying their guns and spraying bullets everywhere. If some seven-foot-tall baddie with gold teeth and skull tattoos came out of the house, no way was I going to be trapped in a police car.

As the seconds turned into minutes, and the minutes dragged by without any sign of action, I could barely restrain myself. How long could it take to search the house? There were only three bedrooms and a bathroom upstairs. And it wasn't like there were exactly a lot of hiding places in any of the rooms.

Finally I slid off the seat and stood next to the car, ready to duck out of sight at the first sign of trouble. Another five minutes had passed with still no sight or sound of Clay or the sheriff. Taking a step toward the house, I cupped my hands to my mouth and called out, "Hey guys, everything okay in there?" I considered adding, "Because I'm still heavily armed, you know," just in case the bad guy had done them in and then thought better of it.

When they didn't answer, I went up to the front porch, scuttling all bent over like you see those SWAT guys do. It was all but impossible to see anything through the darkened front door. "You need any help?" I called. Still no answer.

Now I had a decision to make. The smart thing would be to go back to the road and start heading into town. The sheriff had taken the keys to his car, but I could make it on foot in under an hour. That would be the smart thing to do, but I had never been all that smart when it came to satisfying my curiosity.

Instead I moved up onto the first step of the porch, wincing as it creaked beneath my feet. I shaded my eyes with both hands but still couldn't make out anything through the doorway. I took the next step. If I saw anything—anything at all—I would be gone. I reached the edge of the porch and froze, listening for all I was worth. Not a sound.

Okay, I'd just walk up to the edge of the door, nice and slow, and take a quick peek inside. No matter what, I wouldn't go in though. I'd just creep up softly as a mouse and peek in through the—

Just as I reached the door, a hand darted out from the darkness and clamped around my wrist.

CHAPTER EIGHT

"I thought I told you to stay in the car."

"I . . . I was just . . ." No excuses came immediately to mind as I struggled to get my ragged breathing back under control. I settled on pulling my wrist out from Sheriff Orr's grip and huffing, "You scared the heck out of me."

The sheriff seemed to take satisfaction from my discomfort, which really ticked me off. He studied me with his beady little eyes, as though he'd caught me trying to break into the Pentagon instead of my own grandmother's house.

"Was there anyone up there?" I asked.

He rubbed his jowls as though considering my question. But when he finally spoke it was to ask a question of his own.

"You said you discovered a body in your grandmother's bedroom?"

What kind of question was that? "You mean after all that time you didn't even go up and examine the body?"

He just stared at me with that infuriating look that only police and tax auditors seem capable of pulling off.

"Okay, fine. Yes," I said, willing to play along for the moment.

"And this occurred yesterday between six and seven P.M.?"

"That's what I told you."

"And why didn't you report your discovery until this morning?"

Now I was really getting angry. We'd gone over all this back at the station. "If you want to arrest me for waiting one night, that's fine. But I'd think you might be a little embarrassed by the fact that you've had a dead body sitting under your nose for twenty years without discovering it yourself!"

He scowled at me and scribbled something in a battered notebook he'd pulled from his back pocket. If he thought that was going to intimidate me, he had another thing coming.

"Did you touch anything in the house?" he asked.

"Other than that disgusting body, no," I said. Then I remembered the pictures. "Oh, I also looked at a couple of pictures hanging on the wall."

He scribbled again in his book. This was really getting annoying. "And that's all you touched? The body and the pictures?"

"Yes. Wait, no. I also picked up a music box in Gam's room. I used to play with it as a little girl."

It was as if I'd just told him that I'd been fiddling around with the Holy Grail. His eyes lit up, and he scribbled furiously in his book.

"What's this all about?" I sputtered. "I just want you to get the body out of my grandmother's house."

He tucked the notebook back into his pocket and looked at me as though I were a fly on a pile of cow dung. "I'm going to need you to come to the station with me."

Clay came down the stairs. I turned to him for an explanation. "Does someone here want to tell me what's going on? I only expected to be here for one day, and now I'm going on two. I've got to get back to work, or I'll lose my job."

Clay dropped his gaze as though embarrassed to look at me, but the sheriff shot a stern look at me. "You're not going anywhere but to the station."

I rounded on him. "And *why* would I want to do that?"

"Because at the moment," he said with a scowl, "you're the prime suspect in a murder investigation."

CHAPTER NINE

What is it about authority that immediately makes me feel guilty? Whenever I see a police car in my rearview mirror I drop five miles below the speed limit and start to worry that my registration is expired—even when I've just renewed it. Once, in second grade, I confessed to putting crayons in the teacher's coffeepot, although I'd been at home sick on the day it happened. Forget about being a good liar—I stink at telling the truth.

So of course, as I stood on the front porch attempting to figure how I could possibly be involved in a murder that had taken place when I was learning to jump rope, my hands were trembling, and I could feel myself sweating like crazy.

I swallowed. "Could you please explain what's going on?"

Sheriff Orr studied me, rubbing his cheek with one meaty hand like a baker working a pile of raw dough. "I was hoping you might be the one to do the explaining," he said. "You could start by telling us the name of the dead man we found in your grandmother's bedroom."

"How would I know that?" An image of my grandfather's face flashed through my mind, but I wasn't about to go down that road just yet. "Why don't you ask the guy who left the footprints?"

"See, that's the thing." He pulled a package of toothpicks from his shirt pocket, offered it to me, and when I shook my head, he popped one of the sticks into the corner of his mouth. "It's going to be a little difficult getting much information out of him—since he's dead."

Dead? *Another* dead body in my grandmother's house?

Under other circumstances I would probably have reached that conclusion myself already. After all, it's a reporter's job to put the pieces of a story together, and I consider myself a better-than-average reporter. But these were no ordinary circumstances. I'd felt off balance almost since I arrived in town, and this latest piece of information set my head spinning worse than ever.

"You found *two* bodies?"

"No, just the one," he said. "So far."

"Now I'm confused again." I combed my hands through my hair. Confusion seemed to be my emotion du jour. "You just said that the man who left the footprints is dead. And obviously the body I found hasn't been doing any walking. So . . . what? You're saying someone moved one of the bodies?"

He shifted the toothpick from one side of his mouth to the other. I could hear the wood splintering between his teeth.

"But who could have taken the other body? My footprints were the only ones coming out . . ." All at once it dawned on me. My footprints *were* the only ones coming out. "You think I moved the body don't you?"

He studied me with his piggy little eyes while he ground the toothpick between his teeth. "We searched the house, and there's no other body there."

This was infuriating. I could feel myself beginning to lose my temper. I wanted to grab those jowley cheeks of his and give him a good shaking—which wouldn't do my case any good but would make me feel worlds better. I took a deep breath. "If I moved the body, then why aren't there any other footprints? The only way that could work is if I . . ."

A deep chill filled my stomach, as though I'd just swallowed a gallon of ice water. "If I killed the man who left the footprints."

The sheriff smiled. It wasn't pretty. He held the pencil poised above his pad. "Something you want to tell me? Something you maybe forgot before?"

I stepped down from the porch and began to pace, trying to get everything straight in my head. "Just let me think about this for a minute. There has to be a reasonable explanation. I found the body yesterday, and now it's gone—which means that the man in Gam's bedroom now must have hidden the body I saw."

The sheriff shook his head. "He'd have left footprints if he'd carried a body back out. But he never left the room."

"Okay, okay." I tried to think, but it was hard with him watching me so closely. "He goes to get the body, but somebody else—a third person—follows him up and kills him." The sheriff didn't even bother shaking his head this time. We both knew the footprints ruled that out.

I could feel myself hyperventilating. There had to be a solution, but the more I talked, the guiltier I looked—even to me, and I knew I was innocent.

"Wait. I've got it!" I said, pulling up a tall stalk of grass and waving it at the sheriff. "The guy goes upstairs, gets the body, and throws it out the window. An accomplice takes the body away, but before he does, he shoots his partner."

It was the only thing that made sense, and I was proud of myself for figuring it out. Sheriff Orr didn't share my enthusiasm. "The window was never touched. It doesn't look like it's been opened for years. And the body we found died of repeated blows to the top of his skull. The apparent murder weapon—a wooden jewelry box—is covered with fingerprints you've all ready admitted are yours."

I dropped to the porch steps. If this were happening in an Agatha Christie mystery, Poirot would have the perfect explanation at his fingertips. Unfortunately, this was real life, and I didn't have a clue. "All I can tell you is that I went into Gam's house, found the dead body, panicked, and left."

"At which point you drove into town and ate a hearty dinner?"

It sounded horrible when he put it that way. "I get hungry when I'm stressed. And I hadn't eaten since breakfast. I know I should have come to you right away."

"I think I'd better read you your rights."

I stood, full of indignation. "My *rights*?" An icy dagger plunged into my chest. "You're not really going to arrest me, are you?"

"What did you think we'd do? Issue a citation?" His pale face was only inches from mine, close enough to smell the tang of cinnamon, from the toothpick, on his breath. "Deputy," he said, "place this woman under arrest."

Clay had been in the patrol car talking to someone on the radio. Getting out of the car, he took a pair of handcuffs from his belt. As he passed by, he studiously avoided my eyes. This can't be real, I repeated to myself. *This* can't be *real*.

As Clay stepped behind me, the sheriff ordered me to put my hands behind my back. I heard the rattle of metal and felt cold steel pressed against my wrists. Clay seemed to pause for a moment, muttered something that might have been, "Sorry," and then the handcuffs clicked shut.

"I want an attorney," I whimpered, hoping that this was all just some elaborate gag to teach me a lesson—knowing it wasn't.

The sheriff's face had gone a dusky red. He clamped down on the toothpick, and it snapped it two. "You're going to need one."

CHAPTER TEN

"You did *what?*" The voice on the phone yelped like a kicked puppy.

"I didn't do anything," I groused, my frustration boiling over. A few feet away, Clay appeared to be deeply engrossed in some kind of law magazine, but I knew he was soaking up every word. Fine, let him. I didn't have anything to hide.

"You said you were the one who found the body!" I could picture Bobby Richter's face. My childhood friend was never serene under the best of circumstances, and when he got excited, like he was now, his cheeks became all drawn out and white, while his eyes started doing this odd little jittering thing.

"I said I found a body. Not the body. The body *I* saw . . ." My stomach clenched at the mere thought of the mummified remains I'd touched in my grandmother's bedroom. Swallowing hard, I forced the image out of my mind. "Let's just say my body hasn't done the jitterbug since you and I were flunking Algebra One together in Mrs. Coxson's class."

"So what you're saying is that someone moved the body you found and then killed someone else?" The sound of grinding wheels was nearly audible. Despite our mutual befuddlement with anything mathematical, Bobby's a sharp guy. He entered the police academy right out of high school and passed with flying colors. He is methodical though, which is probably what makes him such a good cop.

"Yes, except . . ." I paused trying to find a way of explaining the footprints without sounding crazy. "Let's just say certain evidence makes them think I killed him." The words sounded so foreign coming out of my mouth—as out of place as the handcuffs Clay had finally taken off my wrists. It would have been funny if not for the fact that I was scared out of my wits.

"I need your help, Bobby. I need you to get me a good lawyer—preferably cheap—but good. And I need you to see what you can find out."

I watched my words carefully, not wanting to get Bobby in trouble. But he knew what I was asking for. He'd done a few favors for me in the past—looking up information that the general public didn't have access to. As a cop, he could get the real scoop on what was happening here.

"Geez, I don't know. I mean, I can find you a lawyer and all. We see plenty of 'em here. But as far as the other stuff . . . This is a homicide investigation."

I'd done my share of favors for Bobby too. So it wasn't like he didn't owe me, but for this one I knew I was going to have to pull out the big guns.

"Okay, then," I paused a moment for effect before dropping my bombshell, "if you've forgotten about Darth."

There was a harsh intake of breath. "No. That's not fair. I've already paid you back for that a hundred times over." I waited silently, knowing I had him.

Garth Braydon, affectionately known as Darth by the kids he terrorized, was the biggest bully at Pleasant Grove Elementary when we were there. Although only in third grade, he could beat up even the toughest of the sixth-graders. This was partially due to the fact that he was one of those freaks of nature who started shaving before turning eleven, and partially because he had been held back two years in a row.

Darth was brutally mean—seizing any chance to smash a kid's teeth into the drinking fountain or to pull a supersonic wedgie on an unsuspecting classmate—while he was at the same time incredibly cagey. He made sure that no adult was ever watching when he made his attacks.

Darth was the ultimate combination of low I.Q., fox-like cunning, and pure, malicious cruelty. We all feared him, but Bobby had the ill-fated luck of being assigned the desk directly in front of him.

I was walking home with Bobby one Friday afternoon, trying not to notice the white elastic band sticking up out of his corduroys, when the idea struck me. I grabbed Bobby by the shoulder. "Do you want to get Darth in trouble? I mean big trouble."

Bobby's eyes began to twitch, but he was nodding. He'd never last the year if we didn't find a way to stop Darth from picking on him.

"It might hurt," I warned.

"So what," he squeaked. "I'm already getting hurt every day." He had a point.

I told him my plan on the way home, and by Monday he was ready to put it into action.

Morning recess was at ten o'clock. When the bell rang, Mrs. Babcock instructed us all to stand beside our desks. Then, one by one, each row filed to the front of the class-room where we lined up to go outside. When it was Bobby's turn, he took one step forward and suddenly fell flat on his face. I grimaced at the sound of his body smacking solidly on the tile floor, but Darth burst into hoarse laughter.

Mrs. Babcock rushed to his side and rolled him over. Bobby's nose and mouth were streaming bright red blood that made me feel all wobbly. "What happened?" she asked before noticing that his shoelaces were tied together. She looked up into Darth's surprised eyes, and for once he was caught off guard.

"I never—" he sputtered. But that was as far as he got. Mrs. Babcock had latched one strong hand onto his arm and lifted Bobby with the other.

"Stay here children," she ordered, dragging Bobby and Darth out the door.

Bobby didn't come back to school until the next day. And even then he was wearing a little silver doohickey with white bandages taped to his nose. We hadn't counted on the fall breaking his nose.

But Darth didn't come back to school for a week. He'd been suspended. And when he did come back, things were not the same. The teachers were gunning for him now, watching his every move. He couldn't get away with so much as a spit wad. His family moved a couple of years later. The last I'd heard of Darth, he'd been suspended from some college football team for drug use.

Years later, Bobby asked me how I'd come up with my plan.

"Well," I said, "Darth never got caught pulling off his attacks. He was too slippery. So it made sense that the only way he was going to get caught was if he wasn't expecting it. He was probably too dumb to grasp the irony, but it was only fitting that after all the times he tied kid's shoelaces together, the one time he got nailed was when the kid had done it to himself."

Standing in this depressing gray office, the cold receiver of a payphone pressed to my ear, I knew Bobby couldn't turn me down. If I hadn't saved his life, I'd at least saved his underwear.

"All right, Shandra, I'll see what I can do. But this really does make us even."

"Thanks, Bobby. You're a sweetheart." I hung up the phone and turned toward the deputy. "Lead on."

CHAPTER ELEVEN

"A maple leaf . . . a rocking chair . . . a three-legged dragon with flames belching from its mouth . . . Elvis Presley wearing the pope's hat . . . that really annoying actor—the one who was in the TV show with Andy Griffith. What was his name? Barney something? He played that goofy police officer . . .

"Oh forget it." I sat up, rubbing bleary eyes with the sides of my balled fists. There was only so long I could entertain myself finding pictures in the cracked and peeling paint of my jail cell ceiling. And besides, the sound of my own voice was starting to drive me bonkers.

Getting up from the ancient cot that could have used a serious dose of Febreze, I approached the gray-painted bars and tried peering far enough out to see the sheriff's office. All I gained for my efforts was the view of a brown desk in the corner and the faint sound of country music.

"Any word from my lawyer?" I called hopefully. I needed him to arrive before they transferred me to the county jail. If anyone heard me, they didn't bother answering. For what seemed like the thousandth time in the two hours I'd been behind bars, I studied the interior of my cell. Three bare walls painted a delicate shade of blah. Oldie-moldy bunk, rust-stained sink, a metal toilet with no lid.

No cable television had appeared since last I looked, no Internet. Not even one of those three-year-old oral hygiene magazines found in finer dentists' offices everywhere. I'd have sold my soul for a Sue Grafton novel.

My stomach growled. Apparently, even incarceration didn't dampen my appetite. I could have lived a happy life without ever knowing that.

"What time is lunch?" I shouted. Again with the silent treatment. This was taking things too far.

"You have to feed me!" I pressed my face against the cold bars. What if there was no one out there? What if they'd all left me alone? I could feel my heart starting to palpitate. It would be just my luck to burst an appendix while I was locked alone in an empty jail. I could starve to death!

"Hey!" I picked up a bar of soap from the edge of the sink and banged it back and forth across the bars hard enough to leave green smudges on the metal. "Is anyone out there?"

"Quiet, girl." The guttural voice came from the cell kitty-corner to my own. I'd assumed it was empty, and the unexpectedness of the words silenced me instantly.

"Cantcha let a fella sleep off his drunk in peace?" A shaggy head appeared over the top mattress of the bunk bed. The reddest eyes I'd ever seen peered at me from a heavily wrinkled face.

"I'm sorry," I said. "I didn't know you were there."

"S'okay." His lips raised in what might have been a smile. His pink tongue poked through the space where his top two teeth should have been.

"Don Knotts," he croaked.

"Pleased to meet you, Mr. Knotts," I said, trying to be cordial. After all, he was the only company available at the moment.

"Not me." His laugh was like rocks bouncing around in a dryer. "Don Knotts is the actor you wuz trying to 'member a piece back. He's right 'tween Elvis and the grinning bovine."

I glanced up at the ceiling. I hadn't noticed it before, but now that he mentioned it, I could clearly see the image of a cow with a ridiculous smile on its face.

"How—"

"Oh, I done my share 'a time in that there cell. Stared up to the ceiling till I wuz dried out 'nuff to stand up." As if to demonstrate the point, he cautiously lifted himself to one elbow and dangled a pair of scrawny legs over the side of the bed. The unmistakable odor of cheap wine emanated from him.

"Lunch's at noon," he said, running a hand across his watery eyes.

I checked my wrist before remembering that they'd taken my watch—along with all my other personal possessions.

"Reckon that's 'bout half a hour." How he could know that after just waking up I had no idea, but I nodded anyway.

"Thanks," I said, my stomach quieting.

"They getcha for lifting?" he asked.

"Pardon me?" Listening to him was like listening to a four-year-old talking around a mouthful of peanut butter and jelly sandwich. All of the words seemed to smash together in one long string of syllables.

He didn't seem the least bit discomfited by my struggles to understand him. I suspected he was used to it.

"I asked was ya brung in for shoplifting." He grinned with wicked delight. "Didn't try an rob that there bank didja?"

"No." I chuckled, unable to help returning his smile.

"That's good." He nodded sagely, tapping the side of his nose with one dirt-crusted finger. "Ain't got enough money there ta make it worth yer while anyways."

He climbed gingerly down from the bed, moving each limb as if it were a stick of fragile furniture. He was wearing a stiff pair of canvas pants and a flannel shirt, both so stained and patched it was impossible to determine their original color. Each had faded to a dull gray that nearly matched the old man's skin.

"If'n ya dint rob no bank 'n ya dint go trying no five-finger discount, whatcha do to get tossed in the calabash?" he grunted.

"I've been asking myself that same question," I said. "I'm not sure I've got the long answer down myself. It's all a little confusing. But the short answer is they think I killed someone."

"Kilt!" The old man had been splashing water from the sink across his face. Now he turned around, droplets of water spilling from his weathered cheeks to leave dark circlets on his shirt. "Who ya kilt?" he asked.

"That's just it. I didn't kill anyone." I don't know why it seemed important to convince an old drunk of my innocence, but it did. I needed someone to believe me. "I was there. I admit that. But the body I saw had been dead for years. I'd have been in elementary school when it happened."

"Dint never kilt no one," he mused to himself, seeming to ignore my words completely. "Wished I did once but never mustered up the gumption."

"I didn't kill anyone!" I could hear the shrillness of my voice but couldn't seem to help myself. "I was just looking around my grandma Brecken's house. Believe me, if I'd known there was a dead body, I would never have gone inside. I wish I'd hadn't even come back. I wish—"

"Elsie's place?" Something I'd said had gotten through to the old man. His eyes were suddenly sharp. He wiped the water from his face with one dirty sleeve.

"Yes," I said, my voice softening.

"You went *inta* Elsie's house?" His eyes were wide, face slack.

"You knew my grandmother." I said. "Do you know anything about the body?"

He raised one trembling finger to his mouth. But before he could speak, there was some kind of commotion from the front of the building. Doors slammed, and a deep voice shouted something I couldn't make out. The sound of footsteps echoed toward us, and without warning Clay was standing in front of my cell.

"What is it?" I asked.

He glanced over his shoulder, where a second man appeared. Clay was tall, but next to the man standing behind him, he looked like a midget. "Your lawyer's here."

CHAPTER TWELVE

Do you remember the scene in *Cast Away* where after hours of struggling, Tom Hanks finally manages to rub together two sticks hard enough to create a spark? Though bloody and exhausted, he dances on the beach, pounding his chest and shouting, "I have created fire!"

That was how I felt when Clay slid my cell door open and I walked out. I'd only been locked up for a few hours, but freedom had never tasted so sweet—even if it only proved to be temporary. Not that I pounded my chest—although I seriously considered it.

"You have my client incarcerated. I request a meeting with her privately." My lawyer's voice was deep and thunderous. He was huge—at least six-eight—and the sleeves of his dark suit jacket looked big enough to wrap around my waist with room to spare.

My first thought was that Bobby had sent Darth Braden as some kind of horrid joke. That thought evaporated as quickly as it had come. Darth couldn't have pronounced incarcerated with a cue card. And while Darth's skin had always been a pasty, unwashed gray, this man's hands and face were a handsome deep bronze.

He stepped past Clay and held out a hand big enough to palm a watermelon. "Teo Inoke," he said. His voice was still deep, but when he spoke to me it seemed gentler, softer. "I'm your lawyer."

My lawyer. Had two words ever sounded so sweet? *My lawyer.* I wasn't alone anymore. Just like that, I felt invincible. If this guy couldn't spring me, he'd bend the bars of my cell and let me walk out.

Bobby, I said silently. *I owe you big time for this one.*

Clay led us to a small, dim room with a coffee-stained table and a small barred window.

"You can leave us now," Teo said. Then, turning to me, he asked, "Can I get you something to drink? A soda? Maybe a candy bar from the machine?" *My kind of guy.* I nodded, and he left the room. In a couple of minutes he was back with orange sodas and Hershey's bars for both of us.

"They're probably stale, but they were the best the vending machine had to offer."

I ripped the paper off my candy bar and crunched into the milk chocolate. To me it tasted like manna.

Teo sat across the table from me, the chair all but disappearing under his bulk. As I picked the last few chocolate crumbs off the wrapper and opened my pop, he pulled a handful of papers from his briefcase. "We probably ought to get a couple of things signed if I'm going to represent you," he said, a smile lighting up his broad face.

I looked quickly over the papers he handed me. They all seemed pretty straightforward until I came to the section that listed his rates and nearly choked on my drink.

"I can't afford this!" I coughed. What he charged by the hour I was lucky to make in three days.

"I'm sorry," he said, sliding the papers back across the table with obvious embarrassment. "I asked my secretary to delete that section." He took an expensive-looking pen from his jacket and inked out the hourly rate. Above it he wrote, *No charge.*

"I don't understand," I said, as he returned the papers to me. Now that I thought about it, his name sounded familiar. I think he was a big shot lawyer out of Salt Lake. He may have been one of the lawyers who handled the Olympics scandal and the Gateway deal. Why was he offering to represent me—and for free?

For a moment the twinkle left his wide brown eyes, and his lips pressed together. "My oldest son made some bad decisions a few years ago. I felt like I had lost him. Your friend Bobby helped me get him back." He smiled again, his white teeth gleaming. "Saula just completed his second year at Stanford."

That sounded like Bobby. He had a way with kids—although it was hard to imagine any child misbehaving with this behemoth for a father. "I don't know how to thank you," I said, signing the papers.

"It's nothing compared to what Bobby did for Saula." He tucked the documents into an expandable folder. "Besides, Bobby said you were innocent. And I agree."

"You may not think so after you see the evidence." I wondered if he'd even be willing to stay on.

"You mean your fingerprints all over the presumed murder weapon? Your footprints in the dust? Or were you referring to the fact that you seem to be the only one who knew the body was there?" He glanced up slyly from a yellow legal pad, where he was doodling something that looked like a tap-dancing duck.

"You know about all that?" I gasped. How had he found out so much so quickly? Bobby? The sheriff? Or did he have some other source?

"Of course." He added a staircase to his drawing.

"And you still think I'm innocent?" I realized that it was supposed be a picture of me going up the stairs in my grandmother's house. He was a lousy artist. I did not look like a duck.

"Absolutely." He added a doorway at the top of the stairs and put a question mark in the middle of it.

"Then how do you explain the footprints?" I asked, fascinated. Maybe this really was going to be like an Agatha Christie story. Except instead of Poirot solving the case, it would be Inoke to the rescue.

"Not a clue," he said, blowing my fantasy out of the water. "Who do you think I am? Columbo?"

I didn't bother correcting him.

"Not to worry." He waved a huge hand at my crestfallen look. "We don't need to know that—yet." He turned the pad so that I could see it.

"We may not know how the murder happened. But we can poke all kind of holes in the theory that you committed it." I was all ears.

"First," he said, making a big black check mark on the left side of the sheet, "the victim was over six feet tall. What are you, five feet?"

"Five-one," I said, sitting up straight. "But what does that have to do with anything?"

"The wounds were on the top of the victim's skull. That would be quite a trick for someone your height, don't you agree?"

"Maybe he was sitting down." I suggested.

He grimaced at me. "Whose side are you on here? Besides, there's more. The medical examiner places the time

of death at a little after eleven last night. The clerk at the
Lazy 8 Motel has you checking in at nine-thirty. He says
your car never left the parking lot."

That's right. I'd told the sheriff I went straight to bed
after dinner, but I didn't think I had any way to prove it.
I'd forgotten that I parked right in front of the motel
office. The kid at the desk had even commented on my
convertible.

"But how could you possibly know that?" I asked. "It's a
three-hour drive up here. You can't have been in town for
more than an hour at the most. Don't tell me you've been
out canvassing the town."

"I have people who work for me. They've been busy this
morning." He slid his untouched candy bar across the table.
"Here. Eat this and listen." I obeyed.

"The only evidence they have against you is circumstan-
tial. And the cops up here haven't done their homework. I'm
willing to bet your prints aren't the only ones on the music
box. If the killer was smart, he wore gloves. But that'd still
leave marks showing that someone else touched it. And that's
if the music box really is the murder weapon at all."

He was very convincing. I could see why he made the
kind of money he did. Inside of me a tiny flicker of hope
sprang up. Maybe I wasn't headed to Attica after all.

He held out one huge hand and began to tick off points
on his fingers.

"You don't fit the height and strength profile of the killer.
You have a fairly solid alibi for the time of the murder. The
police have no idea who the victim even is and certainly have
no motive for you to kill him. There is no physical evidence
tying you to the crime except for your fingerprints on the

music box—which you have an explanation for. And lastly, you're the one who notified the police in the first place."

"So you think I have a good chance of getting out of this?" I asked. The thought of spending weeks or even months inside one of those tiny cells was unbearably horrible.

Somewhere outside the door, the phone rang, and Teo glanced at his watch. "If I'm not mistaken, everything I've told you and more is being passed along to the local constabulary as we speak by a good friend of mine in the DA's office."

"What—"

He stood up from the table. "I hope you haven't become too attached to this place."

"I don't understand," I said, crushing my candy bar wrappers into a brown ball.

Just then the door swung open. It was Sheriff Orr. His face looked especially flushed. He spared Teo a quick glance of disgust before turning to me.

"You're free to go," he grumbled. "But I want you to stay in town."

CHAPTER THIRTEEN

"You know, despite what that blowhard Orr said, you're under no obligation to stay here." Teo and I were standing in the station parking lot between Royce and Teo's sparkling black Mercedes. "It could even be dangerous."

His warning reminded me of what the old man in the pickup truck had said the day before. "I can't leave yet," I said. "Something drove Gam away from the place she loved most. I want to find out what."

He gave me a glare that nearly buckled my knees, but I stood my ground. "You realize that whoever killed the man in your grandmother's house might come after you next," he said.

"What would they stand to benefit from that?" I shook out my hair, relishing the warmth of the sun on my head and shoulders. "Besides, this isn't just curiosity. I need to find out what happened to the other body. I need to prove— to myself at least—that Gam had nothing to do with it."

He set his briefcase on top of his car and folded both arms across his massive chest. "And if the evidence proves she was involved?"

"It won't," I said, trying not to show the sliver of doubt I felt inside.

With a final shake of his head, he reached into his jacket and pulled out a business card. "Call me if you need anything—anything at all."

I'm not normally a very physical person, but after all he'd done for me, I couldn't keep from stepping forward and giving him a big hug. My arms reached barely halfway around his waist. "Thanks," I said.

Being embraced by Teo was like being held by a grizzly. For a moment my feet left the asphalt, and then I was standing on the ground again. I watched him get into his Mercedes and drive away.

Behind me the station door opened. "You're sticking around?"

I nodded without turning. I knew that Clay had only been doing his job, but I couldn't shake the memory of him closing the handcuffs on my wrists.

"You know, you can't go into the house. It's a sealed crime scene."

I tucked my hands into the back pockets of my jeans and watched a minivan pull into the 7-11 across the street. A crowd of kids piled out, screaming for Slurpees and candy.

"I could let you in if you wanted," he added after a minute or two of my silence. "Let you look around or whatever."

I gave him a brief glance. "Actually, I'd like to talk to my jailmate."

"Who?" He looked a little startled that I was talking to him.

"The guy in the cell across from me. The *other* one you locked up." I couldn't help the jab, and I could tell it hit home by his sudden grimace.

"You must mean Trevor Baptista," he said. "He shows up in town drunk once a week or so, and we lock him up until he dries out in the morning."

"I want to talk to him. He seemed to know something about my grandmother." I started walking toward the station.

Clay stepped in front of me. "I wouldn't trust anything Trevor says." He tapped a finger against one temple. "The poor old guy's a little loose upstairs. Besides," he added, "it's too late anyway. He left while you were talking to your lawyer."

CHAPTER FOURTEEN

"What do you mean you're not coming in to work?" Chad shouted. That's the thing I appreciate about my editor—he makes me feel so loved.

"It's only for a couple more days at most." I held the cell phone away from my ear, prepared for another outburst. Chad didn't let me down.

"Do you have any idea what things are like here? I've got a series that's falling apart, a column that stinks like moldy cheese, and an intern that couldn't find the water cooler with a map. Please, tell me you're joking."

While phone service had been nonexistent at Gam's house, it was plenty clear in town. Chad's voice carried so well, the old woman behind the cash register of Echo Lake's general store could probably hear every word. She leaned across the counter, making no effort to hide her interest in my business. I waved, and she grinned happily.

Turning away, pretending to study the limited supply of women's clothing along the back wall, I shielded my conversation as best I could.

"Look, Chad, I wouldn't ordinarily ask you for a favor like this. But the truth is, I found a body in my grandmother's house yesterday. And the sheriff wants me to stick around until they clear everything up."

"A body?" That caught Chad's interest. He could smell a story a mile away. "Do they have a cause of death?"

"Up until about an hour ago, I was the prime candidate," I said, thumbing through the T-shirts in my size. Half of them were emblazoned with Disney characters or the likes of Sponge Bob Squarepants, and the rest sported such original sayings as Where the Heck is Echo Lake? I finally found two plain shirts and tossed them into my basket.

"Really?" I could hear him typing furiously. "So they think it's a murder? Why would they suspect you? Did you get any pictures?"

I filled Chad in on the relevant information while picking out a sweatshirt with the Utah state flag, two pairs of jeans with the give of a cardboard box, and some toiletries. Not exactly the selection of Wal-Mart, but I'm not much into super centers anyway. I have this secret fear that I'll become lost in those labyrinthine aisles, lose what little fashion sense I possess, and be found wandering aimlessly in search of patio furniture.

When I finished telling Chad everything I knew, he thought silently for a minute. "All right," he said. "I can give you two days. But I want a story. And I mean something juicy. Any chance the police there might have set you up? Maybe it's some kind of conspiracy."

Somehow I couldn't picture Clay and Sheriff Orr as criminal masterminds. "No," I said, taking my basket to the counter, "I don't think that angle's going to play out."

"Too bad." Chad's big on political intrigue. He grew up on Woodward and Bernstein, and he's sure that one day he's going to bring down an administration. "Well make sure that it's juicy. And I'm *not* paying for your motel or meals."

"I didn't expect you to." I disconnected and put the phone in my backpack as the woman rang up my purchases.

"Boyfriend?" she asked.

I shook my head. "Boss," I told her, and she gave me a knowing look and smiled.

She glanced at my left hand as she placed my items into a bag. "You know, dear," she said, taking my credit card, "if you're going to be in town for a few days, I've got a nephew I could introduce you to. He sells insurance."

I tried to return her smile. It wasn't easy. "Maybe I'll just pass this time." I took my credit card, stuck my receipt in the bag, and turned to leave.

"All right. But if you change your mind, his office is on the corner of Main and Third South." As I pushed my way through the door, she called out, "I could give him your number!"

Some days it doesn't pay to get out of bed.

CHAPTER FIFTEEN

It's funny. As much as I love water, I've never really been a swimmer. I like to watch it. I like the way it laps softly against the shore, the way it ripples when the wind blows across it, the way the evening sun sparkles off its surfaces as though a million diamonds were hidden there.

Sitting on a hoary downed pine—a tree I'd probably played beneath as a girl—I flicked one last rock out onto the lake. It skipped four times before slipping beneath the dark water.

I'd been sitting on this little stretch of beach below Gam's house for most of the afternoon. I wasn't worried about returning so soon after the murder. Like I'd told Teo, I couldn't see how it had anything to do with me. I'd been in town for less than a day when it happened. I'd come to the lake hoping to get some sense of direction or inspiration. So far, all I had for my efforts was a sore behind and a bunch of burrs in my socks.

As I stood, the stiff new jeans I'd changed into creaked like rusty hinges. Brushing bits of bark and pine needles from my legs, I stared up at the roof of Gam's house—just barely visible through the woods that covered the hillside between the lake and the road. Somewhere between the lake and the house was a trail.

Gam used to name the wild flowers for me as we would follow the winding path down to the water's edge. Although she knew their real names, I loved it best when she made them up. "Look, Shandra, those are Unicorn's Tears. If you tuck a sprig behind your ear before you go to bed, you'll dream of your true love."

Being at Gam's had been like entering my own personal fairytale—a way of escaping the increasing tension between my mother and father. Now, watching the bright blue water shimmering in the late afternoon sun, I could almost hear her voice again—could almost pretend that I was still six years old. Then a deep melancholy settled heavily on my shoulders.

I wouldn't be hearing Gam's stories again—would never take her wrinkled hand in mine as we went for long walks. She had single-handedly raised my brother, Steve Jr., and me after our mother died. Was it possible the woman I thought I knew so well had known about the body? Or had she actually killed someone?

I couldn't bring myself to believe that the kind, loving, soft-spoken woman I knew could ever hurt another human being. I couldn't even remember her raising her voice in all the years she'd lived with us.

"So, Gam, you have any advice?" I asked no one. Not surprisingly, I didn't get an answer.

Unable to find any trace of the old trail, I'd been forced to fight my way down to the water's edge through many years' worth of underbrush and fallen branches. I set off at a diagonal through a grove of aspen that looked more passable. Sitting by the lake, I'd come up with a rough plan of action. I needed to find out as much as I could about the weeks before Gam left. The most likely sources would be any longtime residents who were still around. Finding them might take a little work.

As the sun dipped low in the sky—its edge brushing against the tips of the western slopes—a cool breeze kicked up off the water. The smell of the lake, deep and a little intoxicating, was wonderful, but I wished I hadn't left my jacket in the car. At the edge of the aspens, I came up against an impenetrable deadfall of branches wedged against a rotting log and had to backtrack a ways to get around it.

I hoped to locate Pete and Trevor first. Both had been affected by my appearance at Gam's house. Hopefully one or both of them knew something that might help me.

Now I was deep enough into the woods that I couldn't make out the lake behind me or the clearing at the top of the hill. Not that there was any worry of getting lost. As long as I kept climbing, I would eventually hit the road. But with daylight quickly fading, it was a little creepy being out there by myself. I thought about Teo's warning. Standing in the afternoon sunlight, only a few feet from the sheriff's station, it had seemed laughable. Now it didn't seem quite so funny.

I redoubled my efforts to walk faster, bending forward with my hands on the tops of my thighs, realizing with each step how out of shape I was. A little to my left I spotted what looked like a path of some kind. Remnants of the path Gam and I had walked, maybe? The path was relatively clear of brush and seemed to head in the right direction.

Following the trail made things much easier, and I was able to catch my breath. The top of the hill couldn't be far now. No more than a few hundred yards at the most. I'd wandered farther to the left than I meant to, but once I reached the road it wouldn't take me any time at all to—

With my eyes focused on the trail, I hadn't been watching where I was going. It wasn't until I entered a clearing that I looked around and saw the cold remains of a campfire and a battered cooking pot on a rock beside it.

I turned slowly around. A few feet from the fire, sticking out from an old log was a large hunting knife. Something dark and sticky-looking covered the blade. Above the knife, a tattered pair of socks and a faded flannel shirt hung from a length of rope. On the other side of the clearing, a lean-to made out of canvas and tree branches was almost perfectly camouflaged. Someone had been living there. Recently by the looks of it. Were they still here?

Behind me a twig cracked, and I wheeled around. I couldn't see anything, but in the dim light the woods were a maze of shapes and shadows. Something crashed through the bushes to my right. I almost jumped out of my skin.

The realization of just how isolated I was shot through me like a bolt of lightning. No one had any idea where I was. If anything should happen—

A loud crash like a falling tree hitting the ground echoed through the woods, and for a second I froze in panic. I had to get out of here—back to the lake or through the camp and up the hill. I started toward the trail and stopped. Bad idea. If I went to the lake, I'd have to come up the hill again anyway. Only by then it would be completely dark.

I turned and took two steps toward the other side of the clearing before my legs stopped moving. My throat clamped down like a vise as my heart tried to leap up through it. All the energy seemed to drain from my body, and although I could feel a cry trying to come out, no sound escaped my lips.

Standing in the woods, almost completely hidden by the shadows, someone was watching me.

CHAPTER SIXTEEN

For a moment we both stood frozen. Although less than twenty feet separated us, I could make out little more than his outline in the quickly fading light. A tiny squeak managed to escape my lips, something between a cry and a moan. The sound seemed to break both of us from our stupors. He took a step toward me. I turned and ran.

There are times in our lives—moments that come back later to haunt us—when rational thought proves impossible. Racing down the hill, I operated on pure instinct. Several yards along the trail I randomly cut into the woods. In my panic I didn't notice the branches slapping my cheeks and arms.

At a thick stand of brush I was forced to dart to the left, heading slightly up the hill again. There was no reason or direction to my flight, only the pressing need to escape. The pounding of my heart drummed huge in my ears, but not loud enough to block out the sound of someone crashing through the woods behind me.

Catching a narrow tree trunk with one hand, I swung back to the right. I hazarded a quick glance over my shoulder and saw that, although he was no closer, the figure was still behind me. He might have called something out, but if so, I couldn't understand it over the roaring in my head.

I faced forward again just in time to see an outcropping of rock appear directly in front of me. With no time for thought I leapt into the air and felt the jagged surface of the granite scrape against the bottoms of my shoes. For a second I nearly lost my balance—pinwheeling my arms to keep from falling—and then I was past it.

I have no idea how long I ran or how far—only that I raced through the woods, mind numbed with fear, until my lungs burned and my legs trembled with every step. I hadn't dared to look back again, terrified that my pursuer would be right behind me, but I was sure I could hear his footsteps. The light had almost disappeared from the sky, making it harder and harder to see where I was going or who might be following me.

I don't exactly remember running into the tree. One minute I was on my feet and the next I woke up lying crumpled on the ground. I had a blurry recollection of turning at the last second to avoid some dark shape—of searing pain racing down the right side of my face and through my shoulder to my fingertips.

When I regained consciousness, it was completely dark. It took me a while to realize where I was and how I'd come to be there. My T-shirt was damp with perspiration, leaving me cold and shivering, but my heart was no longer racing, and my breathing had slowed to almost normal.

I lay perfectly still, afraid to move, fearful that he was still out there looking for me. Off to my left I heard something pass through the bushes in the darkness. I clapped my hands to my mouth trying not to make a sound. It came again, the stealthy crackle of breaking twigs, the rustle of leaves, and then nothing. *Him? Or some wild animal?* I was in no hurry to find out either way.

When several minutes had passed with no further sounds, I allowed myself to sit up. My head felt as though I'd been on the Disneyland teacup ride for way too long, and for once I didn't feel that my stomach was capable of holding down anything more than a couple of Extra Strength Tylenols. I explored my right temple, where the worst of the pain seemed to originate, and instantly pulled my fingers away from a nasty bump.

That was going to look attractive in the morning—assuming that I made it out of this alive to see the morning. Now that my fear had abated a little, I tried to assess my condition. Although my legs felt like I'd just completed the St. George Marathon, nothing seemed to be sprained or broken. My right shoulder complained loudly when I moved it, and both my arms were covered with welts and scratches, but nothing was broken.

I turned my head carefully, trying to get some idea of where I was. Distantly I thought I could see moonlight sparkling off the surface of the lake. There were other houses in that direction—phones to call for help. Still, the nearest of those was at least a mile away, and I wasn't up to any long hikes through the dark. I didn't think the road at the top of the hill could be more than a quarter mile off.

Even after I'd made the decision to try and reach my car, I continued to sit by the tree. A picture had formed inside my head; a dark figure crouching motionless only a few feet away, watching and waiting for any sign of movement. The image was paralyzing in its strength. The longer I sat there, the more real it became. Every gust of wind was his hushed breathing—every crackle or groan, the sound of his footsteps.

Finally I realized that if I sat there much longer I would literally become incapable of moving. It was the idea of me sitting alone by the side of this tree all through the night, frozen with terror and indecision that finally got me moving. Gritting my teeth, adrenaline coursing through my veins, I rose slowly to my feet.

Taking a deep breath, I placed one foot in front of me. The sound of my footstep seemed thunderous. I waited, sure that at any second someone would spring out from the darkness. When nothing materialized, I took a second step. That one didn't seem quite so bad. At least if I was this easy to hear, I rationalized, he would be too.

My journey up the hill was a constant battle of fear and frustration. Every tree transformed itself into a human shape preparing to lunge at me, every branch a hand reaching out. Each time I felt I was finally making some headway, an impassable blockage of trees and brush forced me to backtrack.

It wasn't until I dropped down into the drainage ditch by the side of the road, twisting my ankle and almost falling, that I realized I had finally made it.

As I stepped up onto the gravel, clouds drifted in front of the moon, plunging the road and the woods on either side of it into almost total darkness. Hands held out in front of me, I began shuffling in what I hoped was the direction of Gam's house.

At the thought of getting back to my trusty little Royce, I picked up my pace from a hitching limp to a daring bolt. Reaching into my pants pocket, I panicked for a second when I couldn't feel my keys. No, there they were. It was just hard to feel them through the stiff fabric of my new jeans.

As I rounded the curve in the road, I thought I could just discern the outline of Gam's house. I was so intent on reaching my car, on getting back into town, that I didn't see the man standing in the middle of the road until I was almost on top of him.

CHAPTER SEVENTEEN

"Get away from me!" I screamed. I tried to run past him, but the man caught me by the shoulders.

I spun inside his grip and balled my fist.

"Hey—" he started. Before he could say anything else I slugged him in the eye. He fell back a step, his hands dropping, and I turned to run.

"Geez, Shandra, what was that for?"

I paused, staring at him through the darkness, ready to break if he made another move for me. He turned, rubbing his eye, and the moon caught him full on.

"Clay?"

"You punched me!" It was Clay. "You punched me in the eye!"

"What are you doing here?" I asked, lowering my fists.

"I could ask you the same thing." He stepped toward me, probing at a spot under his right eye with one finger. "I drove by and saw your car parked in front of the house. I saw that you hadn't gone inside, so I decided to wait. When it started to get dark and you hadn't shown up, I got worried and went looking for you."

As he drew nearer to me, he stopped rubbing his eye and stared. "What happened to *you*?"

In my fear I'd forgotten about the lump on my head. Now that he'd mentioned it, the pain came back with a wallop. "I, uh . . ."

For some reason I didn't want to tell him about the man I'd seen. Maybe I was still bothered by the fact that he'd put me in jail, or maybe I just wanted to handle things on my own. The last thing I wanted was Clay and the Sheriff searching through the woods for what would probably turn out to be a poor homeless man whom I'd overreacted to.

"I ran into a tree."

He reached toward my face, and I flinched away, expecting him to jab roughly at the bump. Instead his fingers were gentle and slightly cool against my skin. He brushed back my bangs. "You should really get that looked at." His fingers found the scratches on my face. "What did you do— climb through a blackberry bush?"

"I must have scratched myself hiking up from the lake."

In the silvery light I could see his mouth drop into a skeptical frown, but if he questioned my story, he didn't say so. Instead he hooked his thumb toward the police cruiser that I could now see parked just past my car. "Let me give you a ride into town. Doc Rumstead can take a look at you and make sure you don't have a concussion or anything."

"No, that's okay. I'm sure I'll be fine in the morning." Smiling hurt my face, but I tried to grin anyway. I didn't want him worrying about me, and I didn't want to go to a doctor who would probably tell me I needed a tetanus shot or something equally heinous.

"Then at least let me take you over to Mike's. Nan can get you some ice and a couple of aspirins." He closed one hand on my elbow and began walking me toward the cars. I did not want to go into a crowded restaurant looking like I did, but I had the feeling I wasn't going to be able to talk him out of looking after me. It was kind of nice.

"All right, but I'm taking my own car."

"I'll follow you," he said. But I thought I heard him mutter something under his breath that sounded like, "Stubborn." That was okay too.

CHAPTER EIGHTEEN

"Should I dial 911 to report police brutality or resisting arrest?" Nan called out as Clay and I stepped into Big Mike's. She was the waitress who had served me the other night. Beneath the diner's bright fluorescent lights I could see a dark purple crescent under Clay's eye where I'd punched him.

"Sorry about that," I said, grimacing.

"It's okay." He stuck out his chin. "It makes me look tough." I headed to the ladies' room while Nan grabbed a couple of menus and walked Clay to a booth near the jukebox.

Standing in front of the mirror, I realized that no amount of foundation was going to keep me from looking like I'd just gone three tough rounds with a food processor. The bump on my head had a rainbow of dark colors surrounding it that would have done Crayola proud. I settled for brushing the leaves and twigs out of my hair and hiding the smaller scratches with a touchup stick.

When I got back to the table, Clay was gingerly holding a plastic baggy filled with ice to his eye. Another bag was sitting on the table, along with a glass of water and a plastic bottle of Motrin.

I swallowed two pills, and Clay pressed the bag to my head. "Ouch," I squealed, pulling the ice away.

Clay grinned. "We look like a couple of survivors from the Alamo."

"I don't think anyone survived the Alamo," I said, reapplying the ice more carefully.

"Good point." He studied his menu for a minute. "Are you hungry?"

I shook my head. "My stomach's still a little queasy."

"Yeah, I don't feel much like eating either." He closed his menu and stared at me so hard it made me nervous. Just when I was about to slug him in the other eye, he said, "What really happened out there tonight?"

I shifted uncomfortably on the vinyl bench. "I don't know what you're talking about."

"Come on. When you saw me standing there in the road, you looked like you'd seen a ghost. And then you shouted, 'Get away from me!' Are you going to try to tell me that's normal?"

I shrugged. Part of me wanted to tell him everything that had happened—wanted to have him tell me that he'd round up a posse and catch the mysterious stranger in the woods. But then I'd have to explain how I'd lied to him about my injuries.

"I guess I got lost. I heard something in the woods, and it spooked me a little."

"What kind of something?" he asked. I was saved from having to come up with an answer by the appearance of our waitress.

"That ice helping any, kids?" she asked. Clay and I nodded. He waved his hand from me to her. "Shandra," he said, "let me introduce you to Nanette Huffington, best grub slinger and part-time medic in seven counties."

Nan held out her hand. I shook it with the hand that wasn't holding my ice bag. "Pleased to meet you," I said.

"Nan," Clay said, swinging his hand back in my direction, "Shandra Covington. Best middleweight boxer and . . ." he paused, looking at me. "I never asked you what you do."

"I'm a reporter for—" I never got to finish my sentence, because I was suddenly and painfully pulled into a bear hug by Nan.

"Shandra! Shandra Covington—of course! I should have recognized you the first time you came in, but you're all grown up." She pulled back to look at me and then yanked me into another embrace. This time I managed to get my ice bag out of the way.

Clay looked as surprised as I did. "You know her?" he asked.

"Course I do." The gray-haired waitress bubbled. She released me again, and I held out the ice bag to forestall any further attacks. "This is Trinny's little girl."

Now it was my turn to be shocked. Trinity Covington was my mother. The only people I'd ever heard call her Trinny were Gam and my father.

"You knew my mother?" I asked.

"I sure did." Nan looked like she wanted to give me another hug. But she managed to hold herself at bay. "Trinny and I grew up together. Why she and I were best friends."

CHAPTER NINETEEN

"You'll lock up when you leave?" a booming voice called out from the kitchen.

"Sure thing, Mike." Nan was wiping up after the last customers had left—a group of teenagers who had covered their table with chocolate milkshake, fries, and a handful of pennies for a tip.

"Okay, then." Big Mike stepped out of the kitchen, apron in hand. He was exactly the opposite of what his name and deep voice implied—not much taller than I was and skinny as a cornstalk. He hung his apron on a hook behind the counter and shut off the kitchen lights.

Flipping the sign on the front door from OPEN to CLOSED, he cast a curious glance at me before waving to Nan. "I'll see you tomorrow, then."

Noticing the way Nan watched him out to his car, I asked, "Are you and he . . . ?"

She grinned, blushing a little around the edges of her high cheekbones, and seesawed her hand in the air. "On again, off again. He thinks I'm too loud, and I've got a thing about guys who can cook better than me. But we're both single and devastatingly attractive, so who knows?"

I silently wished her the best of luck. Personally I would kill for a guy who could cook well.

"Let me wash up a minute, hon," she said, giving the table a final swipe.

"Not a problem," I waved my fork in the air as though impatience weren't eating me up inside.

I'd waited for more than two hours for the restaurant to finally close so I could talk to her. Clay had offered to stay with me, but I knew he needed to be at work in the morning and my motel was only half a block away. So I said good night to him, and he went on his way with a friendly nod.

As Nan disappeared into the restroom, I picked absently at the slice of apple pie she'd given me. I hadn't taken more than a couple of bites. Not that it wasn't delicious—"Fresh apples," Nan had assured me—I just couldn't seem to work up an appetite. The nauseated feeling in my stomach had disappeared, only to be replaced by a swarm of anxious butterflies.

I was actually going to talk to a friend of my mom's. Someone she'd palled around with, maybe even shared secrets with. It was appalling how little I knew about my own mother. Although Gam had been a wonderful mother figure, and I thought the world of her, she didn't like to talk about the past. "Old news is stale news," she always said. "Focus on the future." Over time I'd gotten used to her taciturn nature, accepting it as part of who she was. Now I was wondering if maybe there were a reason she'd avoided discussing her past.

Nan returned, trading her apron for a light sweater. "You didn't like the pie?" she asked, sitting across from me.

"No, it's just that meeting you . . . finding out that you knew . . ." I laid the fork across my plate and turned my head, inexplicably choked up.

Nan placed her long, work-roughened fingers over the top of my hand. Her dark gray eyes were warm with understanding. "How old were you when she died?"

"Almost ten."

"And your brother?" She handed me a napkin that I used to dab at my eyes and nose with. This was so strange, I hadn't cried over my mother since I was a kid.

"He was twelve," I said, trying to get myself under control. "Neither of us took Mom's death very well, especially on top of my father leaving us."

"Steve." Nan's eyes looked out the window over my left shoulder. "I was with Trinny the first time she met your father."

She knew my father, too? Of course that made sense. I'd just never imagined I'd meet someone who could tell me about one of my parents, let alone both. I had a million questions to ask her, but before I could get them sorted out, she gave me a penetrating look and said, "Your brother . . ."

"Steve Jr."

"Named after your father," she said, nodding. "Why isn't he here with you?"

That was a painful subject for me, and I found my hand wanting to shovel pie into my mouth. Instead I busied myself picking crumbs off the tabletop with my fingertip. "We're not that close," I finally said. "We dealt with the loss of our parents in different ways." It was as far as I was willing to go with someone I'd just met.

Nan seemed to understand. She gave my hand a firm, dry pat. "So, what do you want to know?" she asked, tactfully changing the subject.

"Everything!" I blurted out. "What was my mom like? What kinds of things did she do? Did she write? Was she shy around men? What was she like as a little girl?"

Nan's eyes had lit up as I peppered her with questions, her smiling face revealing a hint of what she must have looked like as a young woman. At my last question though, the smile disappeared, her eyes clouding over.

"Elsie didn't tell you much?"

"No," I said, my enthusiasm ebbing into confusion. "She didn't like to talk about the past."

"I don't guess she would." Now it was Nan's turn to study the table for crumbs.

"What?" I asked, taking her hand in mine and squeezing it. "What was Gam hiding?"

Nan's eyes cautiously returned to mine, as if she were taking some kind of internal measurement. "It's not that she was hiding anything." Her words were soft but deliberate. "Some of the things in your grandmother's past—in your mother's past—were painful."

"I don't understand," I said, continuing to grip her hand. What did she mean by *painful*?

"How much do you know about your grandfather?" At her words a sick overlay raced across my mind. Gam's wedding photo from my mother's album—a stern-looking young man in a dark suit and tie—and the face of the dead body I'd found in Gam's bedroom. I shook my head.

"Only that he left when my mother was a girl. Mom never talked about him. Neither did Gam." Hot bursts of pain flared up from my stomach.

Nan squeezed my fingers so tightly it hurt. Her lips moved silently as though searching for the right words.

"Maybe I'm the wrong person to ask," she said. "I don't know what Stewart was like when Elsie first married him. All I know is he was a terrible father to Trinny and a cruel husband to Elsie. He was quick to strike."

"He hit Gam?" Suddenly my fingers felt cold in Nan's grip. I slipped them away.

"And Trinny. She used to show up at school and church with bruises on her arms and legs. Her face, too. And once . . ." Nan's eyes met mine before darting back to the table. "Once Elsie came home and found him . . ."

"Found him what?" Icicles stabbed at my heart and a strange ringing made it hard to hear myself speak.

Nan squeezed her hands together, bony knuckles white. "Trinny couldn't have been any older than eleven at the time. Elsie had been at a church meeting that ran late. When she got home, Stewart's truck was parked in the driveway." Her voice cracked, and she brushed at her eyes. "She found them upstairs. Trinny's dress was torn and she was crying."

"My grandfather did that?" Why had I never heard of this before?

"Trinny could never remember exactly what happened. The house was dark when he grabbed her. But it was clear enough for Elsie. I heard she took an old rifle down from the mantel. It hadn't been fired in years, but that didn't matter to Elsie. She wasn't planning on shooting it anyway." Nan's words, slowly meandering before, now tumbled over one another.

"Her first swing caught Stewart just above the eye. Folks that saw him on his way out of town said it looked like someone had tried to scalp him. The second swing must've caught him a little lower 'cause Mr. Bascom, who ran the filling station, said Stewart could barely walk when he filled his pickup full of gas. I imagine Elsie would've *killed* him if he hadn't run."

Would've killed him. A hundred emotions ran through my brain. Anger, pain, fear, disappointment at never having been told. "That's when he left?"

"Yes. That was when he left. And it was a good thing for him he did. Elsie tried to keep what he'd done quiet. I guess she figured she could handle it herself. But things have a way of getting out in small towns. When the men learned what'd happened, they got together. Word was if he'd ever shown up again, they'd've hung him."

Suddenly I didn't want to hear anymore. I'd had all I could take for one night. There was one question I still had to ask though—one that was very relevant to what was happening now. "*Did* he, Nan?" I whispered. "Did he ever show up again?"

It was like watching a book close. Nan's eyes and mouth, which had been so expressive a moment before, shut down like drawn window shades. She stood up from the table. "I think," she said, pulling her sweater tight around her, "it's time to go."

CHAPTER TWENTY

"What do you mean, it's time to go?"

Ignoring me, Nan swept up my place setting from the table and dropped it on the counter so hard the plate nearly shattered. I could see that her hands were shaking, but she wouldn't look at me as she went around flipping off light switches and pulling blinds closed.

I followed her across the restaurant, left in the dark, both literally and figuratively. "You have to tell me what happened, Nan!" I grabbed her arm. "These are my grandparents we're talking about. Don't you think I deserve to know?"

Nan turned toward me, her eyes reflecting the streetlights outside, her face only a dim shape. "Maybe you do," she said. "But your grandmother chose not to tell you. I'm sure she had her reasons."

"I saw him," I whispered.

"Saw who?" Her voice betrayed no emotion, but I thought I saw a flash of recognition in her eyes.

I moved a step closer, trying to make out the expression on her face. "My grandfather. He was lying dead on the floor of Gam's room."

Nan closed her eyes, her breathing soft as a dropped feather.

"Please, tell me what happened," I begged, my hand tugging the cuff of her cardigan.

"I don't know," she sighed. "I just don't know. Let me think about it tonight, and we'll talk tomorrow."

CHAPTER TWENTY-ONE

There's something about lying on a bed in a cold, austere motel room that makes you feel so alone. Pressing my face against the heavily starched pillowcase, I tried to console myself with the fact that at least I wasn't sleeping in a jail cell. It didn't help much. This tiny cubicle of a room with its sharp edges and barren, white walls seemed a frighteningly accurate metaphor of the way I was feeling.

My head was pounding, and my jaw and neck ached. After leaving Big Mike's, I'd driven down a dark Main Street looking for someplace to pick up more Motrin. Everything was closed. Even the windows of the 7-11 were dark. Whoever heard of a 7-11 that actually closed at eleven? I thought it was like some kind of law that they had to be open twenty-four hours.

So here I was, physically exhausted, knowing that with everything going on in my head, I wouldn't be able to fall asleep for hours. Outside, the wind began howling against the window as if crying to be let in. A few minutes later a steady ticking of raindrops on glass joined the sound of the wind. That was great. The ragtop on my car had been getting progressively worse, and the motel didn't offer covered parking. By tomorrow morning the interior would be sopping.

"Why don't you say what's really bothering you," I said to myself.

Great, I was talking to myself now. Still, I sat up, resting my head on one palm to lessen the pain in my neck. I didn't bother to turn on the light. There was nothing to see. Instead, I stared into the darkness, trying to sort out my feelings.

"My grandfather abused his wife and child and molested his daughter."

Nan's words tonight had shocked me. That was perfectly normal—who could expect to hear something like that about their own relative? And yet, on a deeper level, hadn't I known something was wrong?

Hadn't a part of me recognized the fact that both my mother and my grandmother avoided talking to me about the men in their lives? Hadn't I, at least subconsciously, figured that some dark secret was being withheld from me for *my own good*?

Outside an eighteen-wheeler roared by, shaking the room as it rumbled past like a great brontosaurus. I swung my legs over the edge of the bed and let the soles of my feet swing back and forth on the nubby surface.

Maybe the truth was that I hadn't come to sell my grandmother's house at all. Maybe I'd come in search of a part of myself. Outwardly I'd been focused on a set agenda: go through the house, take some pictures, sign with the realtor, and leave. But inside I'd been half-hoping I might find some clues about Gam's past, my mother's past, and *my* past.

I'd been looking for someone just like Nan—a voice that could help me understand my family. People talk about genealogy every day—about Great Uncle Benjamin, who crossed the plains barefoot, and about Great, Great-

Grandma Jones who bore twins in the back of a covered wagon.

But the things I was learning weren't the things I wanted to hear. Wasn't it bad enough being the daughter of a broken marriage, the granddaughter of a broken marriage, and the sister of a man who might speak to me twice a year? I didn't need any more reminders that relationships weren't my strong suit—I was a twenty-eight-year-old single female in a state where most people view that as unusual and not a few consider it a sin.

What I was discovering about my heritage wasn't pretty. It made me question my already confused understanding of who I really was. The decision I had to make was either to leave while there were still unanswered questions or to take the risk that the truth was only going to get uglier.

As I sat staring into the darkness, an image filled my mind. I saw a short woman standing up to a man who probably scared her to death. Breaking through the years of servility that had been beaten into her, she defended her child. I pictured how she and her daughter had managed to survive on their own in their male-dominated world.

If I found out that my grandfather had come back—that Gam had finished what she started the night she found him with my mother—could I live with that?

"I can live with the truth," I heard myself say. The words sounded good. I just hoped they were true.

Outside, the sound of footsteps echoed on the concrete stairs—some other night owl calling this place home. The footsteps came nearer to my door and then stopped. Suddenly I remembered that I'd opened the sliding window an inch or two that afternoon. Had I closed it when I left? I didn't think so.

A man's voice muttered softly outside the door. *Was it the murderer? Could he be coming after me now?* Without turning on the light, I slipped out of bed and searched for anything I could use as a weapon. The best I could come up with was my shoe. Feeling completely defenseless, I crept up to the window.

I heard the sound the sound of a key rattling into a lock. How had he gotten a key to my room? A rusty doorknob squeaked as it turned. I raised the shoe over my head, and . . . nothing happened. It was the door of the next room over that had been opened.

With a finger of icy perspiration tickling the back of my neck, I pulled back the curtains and shoved the window shut. It snapped closed with a sharp click. As I turned back toward my bed, something caught my eye. A dark shape hung over the back of the chair.

Reaching out with one hand, I touched the soft denim of the jeans I'd been wearing that morning. I'd been too distracted to notice them when I got back from Big Mike's. But I hadn't hung them there. I could distinctly remember tossing them onto the floor when I got back from buying my new clothes.

Had it been the maid? She had come and gone while I was still in jail. Flipping on the light, I looked carefully around the room. Nothing else was obviously out of place, and yet everything seemed just a little off, as though it had all been subtly rearranged.

Someone had been in my room.

CHAPTER TWENTY-TWO

After the day I'd been through, I should have slept like the dead. Instead, I started at every little noise, my heart flittering in my chest like a trapped hummingbird. Knowing someone had been in my room was like shaking a spider out of my shirt. Even though logically I knew the intruder was gone, I kept thinking I heard creeping across the floor or saw movement out of the corner of my eye.

By five in the morning—when I gave up and called the muzzy-sounding desk clerk to ask for a different room—I was a complete wreck. And, of course, by the time I'd packed all of my belongings into a plastic bag, had been drenched by the rain that was still coming down in icy-cold torrents, and had moved into my new room, I was wide awake.

After wrapping my hair in a towel, having checked the lock on my door twice, I lay down on the bed, hoping for at least an hour's rest. Apparently everyone else in the motel had set their alarms for six, because for the next forty-five minutes I was treated to a symphony of clock radios set to artificially cheerful morning news shows hosts, blow dryers that sounded like leaf blowers, and flushing toilets that all seemed to drain into a pipe running directly behind my bed.

Realizing that it was not my lot in life to get another minute's sleep, I pulled on my sweatshirt and jeans and brushed my teeth. I raced out to the car and, jumping in quickly to avoid the rain, sat in a puddle that had formed in the bucket seat. Instantly my jeans absorbed every frigid drop.

This was not going to be my day.

* * *

"I've seen catfish that looked drier than you." Clay was coming out of Mike's as I was heading in.

"I'm sure there's a snappy reply to that," I said, brushing soggy bangs from my eyes, "but I'm either too dumb or too tired to think of it."

Clay blushed. "Not that you look bad or anything. In fact you look really good considering that your hair's all . . . I mean with the rain and . . ." I seemed to be good at discomfiting him. It was kind of fun considering that I'm usually the one doing the blushing around the opposite sex.

"So what you're saying is that I'm very presentable for a total wreck."

"No!" He rubbed a hand along the back of his neck. "Whew boy, maybe we could just start over?"

I considered needling him a little further but decided to give him a break, especially considering that his eye where I'd punched him still looked terrible. "Thank you anyway. That's the nicest backhanded compliment I think I've ever received."

I shook the water from my hair like a wet dog and tried to pull it into some semblance of order. Clay smiled a crooked grin, apparently deciding that I'd let him off easy.

Tipping his head in a way that was severely cute, he held out one hand. "Are we friends?"

I shook his hand—he had nice hands. "Friends," I agreed.

"So, you having breakfast?"

"That was the idea," I said, expecting a food joke.

He didn't take the bait. Instead, he nodded toward the door. "You want to eat together?"

"Didn't you just have breakfast? I assume that's why you were coming out."

"Oh, right." His eyes widened, and again, crimson crept up his neck and cheeks. If I'd known wet, unruly hair and soggy jeans turned cute guys to mush, I'd have spent more time out in the rain.

"Any sign of the other body?" I asked.

He shook his head, resting his hands on his hips. "No. And no word on the identity of the one in the morgue. We're running the prints, though."

"That's good."

"Yeah."

He looked at me as though he wanted to say something, then turned to study the passing cars. "Pretty rainy."

"Yes, it is." We looked at anything but each other, the silence growing awkward.

Finally he reached into his pocket and pulled out his car keys. "You probably ought to go on in."

"Yeah, I'm pretty hungry."

"Okay. I'll see you, then." He started to walk toward the street and suddenly spun around. "Are you seeing anybody? I mean guys. Like a boyfriend or anything?" The words raced from his mouth awkwardly as though he couldn't get them out fast enough. His eyes were glued to the sidewalk.

He was flirting with me. I couldn't believe it.

I shook my head, scarcely trusting myself to speak. "Nothing serious." I could have said not at all and been just as honest. But in certain cases—like this one—it's been my experience that complete honesty is not always best.

"Okay, then. Maybe I can call you sometime." He turned and walked to his car without a second glance, the back of his neck flaming.

Watching him go, I realized I was no longer cold.

CHAPTER TWENTY-THREE

"She ain't here," Big Mike called with an angry scowl, as he stormed out of the kitchen. He carried a coffee pot to a group of white-haired women and managed to slop the hot brown liquid onto the table next to each of their cups as he refilled them.

I assumed he meant Nan, since the only other person serving was a young blonde, balancing at least ten plates on a huge tray as she moved quickly from one table to the next.

"Do you know when—"

"No," he said, cutting off my question. "Said she was sick." He gave me another scowl that left no doubt as to who he was blaming for Nan's absence. I guessed he was probably right.

"You want something ta eat?" he growled. Before I could answer, he slapped a stained menu onto the counter and headed back into the kitchen.

"Chilly, eggs are ready," he bawled. Apparently Chilly was the name of the waitress, because she delivered the last of the plates from her tray, pirouetted with surprising grace and went into the back to load up again. I couldn't have pulled off a turn like that for the life of me.

I slumped onto the stool with a wet squelch. I hadn't bothered changing clothes—knowing that my other pants would get just as wet after sitting on my soaked upholstery. I picked up the menu and began studying it, my jeans producing a steady drip-drip-drip onto the tile floor.

Twenty minutes later, I was working my way through soggy hash browns and a stack of pancakes that looked like someone had used them to put out a grease fire. I wasn't sure whether Nan's absence had thrown off Mike's cooking abilities or if he was just taking his aggression out on me personally.

Sawing at a pancake, I thought about the break-in at my motel room and tried to figure out what the intruder had been looking for. It was a pretty safe guess they weren't there for my soggy sweatshirt or the half-eaten pack of Certs I'd left on the night table. A simple burglary then? Just someone hoping to find a purse or maybe a CD player they could hock?

That didn't ring true either. For one thing, Clay hadn't mentioned any recent motel break-ins when I'd come looking for the sheriff. And for another thing, if it had been a burglar, why wouldn't he have taken the TV or at least the clock radio? No, they seem to have targeted my room specifically, looking for something they thought I might have. But what?

Chilly appeared at my side. "Can I get you anything else?" she asked.

I glanced down at the scrambled eggs on my plate, noticing chunks of what looked like Brillo pad among the lumpy, yellow and white mess.

"A couple of antacids maybe?"

She grinned. "Mike won't admit it, but he misses Nan like crazy when she's not here. It really throws him out of whack." She picked up my plate with a grimace. "How 'bout if I just get you a couple of cinnamon buns and some more juice."

"That would be perfect." My stomach did cartwheels at the thought. Noticing the pink notepad sticking out of her pocket, I asked, "Could I get one of those sheets too? And something to write with?"

"Sure thing." She tore off one of the order slips and handed me a pen with a picture of a burger on it next to the words *Big Mike's—Good Eats.*

As she went to get my pastries, I jotted down everything I'd discovered since coming to Echo Lake.

1. Dead body in Gam's house.

2. Second dead body.

3. Grandpa Brecken molested my mother, and Gam ran him off.

4. Nan won't talk about Grandpa coming back.

5. Someone broke into my motel room.

The list was depressingly short.

I glanced at item number one and added *Grandpa Brecken?* next to it. I didn't know for sure if the dead body I'd found was him, but for now that was as good a guess as any.

Beside the second item I wrote *Who?* and circled it. I had at least a few ideas about how my grandfather's body might have ended up dead in Gam's house, but the other body was a mystery. Apparently Sheriff Orr didn't know any more than I did. I racked my brain trying to think what a complete stranger had been doing in Gam's house after the place had gone untouched for twenty years, and who would want to kill him. Nothing obvious came to mind.

There wasn't much I could do with numbers three or four. But number five held all sorts of interesting possibilities. Next to it I wrote *The man in the woods?* and drew an arrow from that up to number two.

Before I could get any further, Chilly slid a plate in front of me, and all rational thought disappeared in the heavenly aroma of cinnamon and hot bread. When I returned to my senses, the buns were gone and my fingers were covered with sticky goo, but my insides were warm and happy.

Licking the sugar from my fingertips, I checked the list again and thought about possible connections. I couldn't see how any of the items related to each other.

"Mind if I saddle up next to you?" a gravelly voice asked.

I looked from my list into a hard, gaunt face. The man looked as though his weather-beaten skin had been stretched across his cheekbones like a balloon. A dark pair of wrap-around sunglasses covered his eyes.

"Help yourself," I said, trying not to stare.

His gaze went from my straggly hair to my steadily dripping jeans that had left a puddle reaching to the stools on either side of me.

"Sorry about the water," I muttered.

"Ought to get yourself an umbrella." As he sat down, he took off his glasses and I couldn't help from gasping softly.

He had the creepiest eyes I'd ever seen. They were the lightest shade of blue and shiny like metal. Looking at them was like looking at a painting of eyes—they seemed to have no life at all.

"Problem?" he asked, his lips barely moving as he spoke.

"No." I turned away, drinking my juice and trying to ignore the stench of unwashed skin and stale cigarette smoke drifting over from him. He ordered a doughnut and a cup of coffee.

"What's your name?" he asked, sending a puff of rancid breath in my direction.

"Shandra," I said without looking into his eyes.

He dumped several tablespoons of sugar into his coffee, tasted it, and dumped in a little more.

"Once knew a girl named Shandra." He dunked a doughnut into his coffee and took a big squelching bite. "She's dead now."

Okay this was just a little too bizarre. I looked around, hoping that Chilly was somewhere in the vicinity so I could pay my bill and beat a quick exit, but she'd gone into the kitchen. Fortunately the man—perhaps deciding I wasn't his type after all—pulled a newspaper out of his pocket and disappeared behind it.

Relieved to have his frightening gaze off me, I glanced at the paper he was reading. It was one of those thin jobs, printed all in black and white. The lead story was about an upcoming blood drive, but it was the masthead that caught my attention—THE WEEKLY ECHO. And in smaller print—*Covering Echo Lake for over Fifty-Five Years.*

Unexpectedly the paper dropped, and I found myself staring into his eyes. It was like being watched by some kind of poisonous desert reptile. Before I could turn away, he slid the paper across the counter to me. "Interesting story here."

I looked down. The headline read, *Salt Lake Woman Charged with Murder.*

CHAPTER TWENTY-FOUR

Ching-ching. A small silver bell announced my arrival as I walked through the door and into the offices of the *Daily Echo*. The smell of newsprint and ink brought back a host of memories from my early days as a reporter. At the office I work in now, the closest most reporters get to the finished product is when we pick up a copy in the lobby of our downtown office building. The actual printing and circulation take place on the other side of town. But at the *Twin Forks Gazette,* I'd followed the papers all the way from writing them to pulling the bundles out of the back of the delivery truck.

Not that a paper the size of the *Daily Echo* would do its own printing. They probably used a press in Salt Lake as well. But all along the front window, I could see bundled stacks of fresh papers waiting to be picked up by the carriers. It was the scent of the bundles—still hot off the press, as the saying went—and that of the thousands that had been there before them that filled the air.

"Can I help you?" It took me a second to spot the face peering at me over the edge of a nearby cubicle. My heart dropped when I saw who was speaking. The kid couldn't have been any older than nineteen or twenty—probably not even born during the time period I was looking for. He had wide, curious eyes, and a chewed pencil was tucked behind his ear.

"I wonder if I could speak with your managing editor," I asked, crossing my fingers in the hope that someone worked there who was a little older than him.

"That's me," he piped, coming around to the counter. Rats, I should have crossed my toes, too. I handed him my business card, counting on my credentials as a senior reporter for the *Deseret Morning News* to buy me a little clout. His next words burst that balloon.

"You aren't looking for a job are you?" he asked, his pale lips pulling down into a frown.

"No," I said hastily. "I just had a couple of questions."

"Whew." He wiped his brow. "My grandma would fire me in a minute if she thought there was a real reporter to take my place."

"No need to worry on my account."

"Well, that's good," he said, the grin returning to his face. "Since you're not here for my job, let me introduce myself."

He leaned across the counter and held out his hand. "Chris Stevens. I write, sell ads, and do layout."

"Shandra Covington," I returned, gripping his bony fingers. "Been there, done that."

He looked at me and then down at my card again. "Hey, you're the one . . . the one . . . they arrested for killing that guy at the old Brecken place."

"I think *arrested* might be a little too strong," I muttered, feeling the color blossoming on my cheeks.

"No, no. I took the information myself." Chris ran around the counter and pulled one of the papers from the top of a bundle. He opened to the second page and pointed to the headline. *Salt Lake Woman Charged with Murder.*

I was definitely *Salt Lake Woman.*

"Do you mind telling me how you got that information?" I asked, sure he was going to cite confidential sources, as I would have done.

Instead, he seemed only too excited to help out. "Sheriff Orr told me all about it." Well that answered *that* question. Apparently the sheriff wasn't a forgive-and-forget kind of guy. I'd have to remember to thank him.

"Since I'm not in jail. It would seem the sheriff misspoke, don't you think?" I wished the kid would quit staring at me like I was some kind of celebrity. If the weight of a gaze could cause hives, I'd be breaking out in red lumps all over.

"So who was the guy?" he asked, ignoring my response entirely. "Some kind of criminal or something?"

"Look I'd really rather not discuss that," I said. "I was kind of hoping I might be able to get some information on my—" I nearly said grandmother before biting back my words. "That is, I'm looking for information on what Echo Lake was like around, say, the early 1980s."

"Was the victim blackmailing you?"

"No," I said, trying to get his mind off of my arrest. "I'd like to see some of your past issues. Do you have them on microfiche?"

"Nope." He scratched at a pimple on his forehead. "Just the stacks. I'll tell you what. You tell me the name of the guy you killed, and I'll help you find your information."

"I really don't know anything about the man they found," I said, taking a few steps toward the door at the back of the room. "Now, if you could just show me where you keep your old copies?"

"Are you looking for the goods on that guy? 'Cause I could help you find stuff in exchange for an inside scoop on the story—like why you whacked him."

I could see this was going to go on all day if I didn't do something desperate. Fortunately I thought I knew just the thing to shut him up. Gambling that he was Mormon, I opened my eyes a little too wide, and feigning a look of complete innocence, I asked, "So, when are you going on your mission?"

Before the sentence was halfway out of my mouth, the look of sullen rebelliousness I'd been hoping for appeared on his face. I'll bet he'd heard that question a hundred times or more over the last twelve months. *Sorry, kid,* I said silently. *I feel exactly the same way about the "When are you getting married?" question.*

"I just need to finish filling out my papers," he grumbled.

"Do you have enough white shirts and ties?" I asked, twisting the knife just a little deeper, "because you can really never have too many white shirts and ties. I hear Mervyn's has them on sale."

That did the trick. His mouth dropped, and he led me to the back room, forgetting all about our previous conversation.

As I followed him into a dimly lit storage room filled with piles of cardboard boxes that reached above my head, I thought about asking him if he'd memorized all his *missionary discussion scriptures,* but that would have just been gratuitous.

CHAPTER TWENTY-FIVE

In the movies they always make research look so exciting. The hero spends at most a couple of hours—and usually it's only twenty or thirty minutes—flipping through ancient manuscripts before the *aha* moment occurs. The camera pans in close and Indiana Jones goes, "Aha! I know where the Holy Grail is hidden."

Reality is nothing like that. Ask anyone who does a lot of research for a living—a reporter, lawyer, or the ever-popular private investigator—and they'll set you straight. Mostly research is hour upon hour of fruitless, eye-straining reading, rewarded more often than not by . . . nothing.

By one fifteen in the afternoon I was tired and sore but no closer to any information about my grandparents than when I'd started. My clothes were finally dry, although now I was covered from head to foot with a fine dust made up of equal parts powdered news print and years of dirt, with a sprinkling of cobweb thrown in for good measure.

Nearly all newspapers have a morgue. That's newspaper lingo for where the old issues are stored. With the advent of microfiche, the morgue doesn't get accessed that often anymore. And when you do need to find a physical copy or an original photograph, the morgue is a clean, well-

organized space where everything is indexed for your conve-
nience.

What I was searching through here was not a morgue under
any sense of the word. It was a storage room plain and simple.
The closest thing to indexing was the occasional felt-tip
pen–scrawled date on the outside of a box that might or might
not identify the issues stored inside.

After hours of painful bending over old papers and
straining my back reaching for boxes, I had learned many
things.

Echo Lake has a celebration for every occasion—most
include a potluck or bean supper. Ethel Vanderneed-
Roberts—a direct descendent of Thomas M. Vanderneed,
founder of Echo Lake—has tried and failed to get a statue
erected in her progenitor's honor on at least six separate occa-
sions. And last, but—according to the amount of coverage
given it—not least, Velma and Gordon Lydell have won
Echo Lake's most beautiful yard award more times than you
can shake a lavender teagarden rose at.

Mundane as all that sounds, under most circumstances
I'd find this stuff of at least passing interest, and at times
even fascinating. One of the things that drew me to jour-
nalism in the first place was the allure of peeping into other
people's lives—finding out what makes them laugh and cry.
I'm an information rat, storing away tidbits of knowledge
like seeds and nuts for a rainy day.

But I'd come here with a specific purpose in mind, and
after all the pages I'd pored over, the only story mentioning
either of my grandparents was one in which Gam's name was
listed among a group of women cooking at the annual
Fourth of July breakfast.

The one piece of useful information I'd come across was the last name and address of Pete, the old guy who had stopped to talk to me in front of Gam's house. Courtesy of a picture taken of him at his June 1984 barn raising—complete with bean supper, thank you—I knew that he was Pete Blackwood of 2204 Hammer Lane. He would be my next stop.

I gathered the current pile of newspapers off the rickety old card table I'd been using as a desk, loaded them up, and returned the box to its stack. Rubbing the dust from the face of my watch, I figured I had time for two more boxes before my stomach and brain conspired together to go on a hunger strike.

According to my list, I'd covered May 1983 through December 1984, all of 1963 through 1966, and half a dozen of the years between. My primary focuses had been the time period shortly before Gam left Echo Lake and the approximate date Gam had run my grandfather out of town. I decided to try 1961 through 1962 for no other reason than I hadn't done those years yet.

With a silent curse for whoever had created this disordered mess, I began to work my way from isle to isle, wiping the dust from each carton and straining to read what was scribbled on the side. Trying to decipher the chicken scratch made my eyes burn. The only light came from a pair of sixty-watt bulbs hanging from the ceiling and a single small window so dirty I couldn't tell whether it was still raining outside or not.

Near the back of the room, I found the box I was looking for. Of course it was at the top of the stack. Stretching my five feet one inch as high as I could, I grabbed either side of the carton and pulled it toward me. As the box teetered precariously, a thick layer of dirt and something that smelled suspiciously like mouse droppings rained down onto my upturned face.

Trying not to inhale any of the debris, I somehow managed to wobble back to the table, where I dropped the box with a thud. Another dust cloud rose into the air. Pulling the top of my shirt up over my mouth, I glanced toward the window. It looked as though it were sealed closed by several layers of old paint, but getting a little fresh air into this musty space would be well worth the effort.

As I walked toward the window, I thought I saw a flash of movement. Was someone out there? Cupping my hands to the dirt-grimed pane, I could barely see a brick wall a few feet away but nothing more. I turned the small brass catch and shoved up on the frame. For a moment nothing happened. Then, with a tooth-grinding squeal, the glass rose six inches before freezing in place.

Peeking through the opening, I could make out the rain-darkened pavement of a narrow alleyway outside. Two garbage cans that had seen better days leaned drunkenly against one another amid a pile of old cans and newspapers. One end of the alley was closed off by a high chain-link fence. I couldn't see the other end, but I assumed it opened into the street. If there had been anyone out there—and with all the gunk on the window, it was impossible to tell if I had seen anything or not—they were gone now.

I took a deep breath of the cool, rain-fresh air through the crack and was just turning away from the window, when something leaped out from behind one of the trashcans. With a gasp, I stepped backward, nearly tripping over a box of papers. Outside the window a shadow moved. I took another step back just as a face dropped down to the opening and peered in at me. It was . . . a cat.

"Oh for pity's sake," I said, trying to get my heart rate back to normal. Below the window a pair of green eyes stared out at me from an orange and white-striped face.

"You scared the bejeebers out of me," I groused. "That was exceptionally rude."

"Meowww," replied the cat in a tone that sounded far more amused than conciliatory. I'm not much of a cat lover by nature, and this member of the feline family did nothing to change my mind. I made a waving motion toward the window, and he disappeared. Favoring the ankle I'd banged, I returned to the table.

The newspapers inside the box had turned from white to a dirty yellow. The masthead was in a different typeface than the newer issues, but other than that, everything looked the same. Working my way from issue to issue, it seemed that I was reading the same news over and over.

Where were the headlines? Kennedy had been elected president and was only a few months from facing the Cuban Missile Crisis. The U.S. was coming ever nearer to sending troops into Vietnam. People were building bomb shelters in their backyards. But from what you could read in the *Daily Echo,* all of that was upstaged by who made the best jelly at the county fair. It was as though Echo Lake was a world unto itself.

I flipped from page to page, barely seeing the stories that flashed in front me. I don't know why I was so angry at inane story after inane story, but I *was* angry—*furious* at the complaisance of this little town. I was turning pages so quickly I nearly missed his picture when I came to it.

I was two pages past when my mind matched the photograph of the men standing in front of some kind of building with the pictures I'd seen of my grandfather. I turned back to the image. He was wearing a leather tool belt over a pair of saggy jeans. A cap was pulled low over his eyes, but there was no question of who it was.

He was standing with three other men in front of what must have been a fairly modern building at the time—a lot of glass and brick. The caption below the picture read, *New Zions Bank building nearing completion.*

As I ran my finger over his face, a shadow dropped across the newspaper, and a voice said, "I see you found him."

CHAPTER TWENTY-SIX

Startled, I looked up into a woman's face that was all lines and angles. No-nonsense silver-framed glasses hung from a nose as straight as a carpenter's level. The gray eyes behind the lenses were intense. Her features looked sharp enough to slice through paper, and her hair was pulled back from her face in a perm so tight you could almost hear it scream.

I'm usually not intimidated by people—self-conscious yes, especially around men, but not intimidated. Still, something about this woman unnerved me. Maybe it was the way she perched over me like a vulture or how her cold eyes studied me without blinking.

"I see you found him," she repeated.

"He's my grandfather."

"Yes, I know." She took the newspaper from my hands, folded it, and placed it back with the others. "Are you finished here?"

I looked down at the few notes I'd taken and then at the seemingly countless number of cardboard boxes surrounding me. "I think I am."

"Well then, come with me," she said, turning with the precision of a general. She was dressed in a pantsuit made of some sort of glistening black material that sparkled when she moved—the kind of outfit only a woman over sixty could get away with. With her coif of silver hair and the jeweled chain attached to her glasses it went perfectly.

Acutely aware of my own filthy clothes, I put the stack of papers back into the box and started to pick it up.

"Just leave that. It'll give my grandson something worthwhile to do," she said. "You met Chris when you came in?"

"Yes." Although if I'd met the two of them on the street, I'd never have guessed they were related. They looked nothing alike.

Seeming to read my mind, she rolled her eyes in an expression that showed both irritation and endearment. "He's a dear boy but rather scattered—like his parents. They asked me to give him a job. Try to whip the boy into shape. So far it isn't working, and neither is he."

As we reached the door, she glanced back into the gloom. "Have you deciphered my filing system?" she asked.

For a second I considered lying, and then just shook my head. "No," I admitted. "Not at all."

Gradually a smile appeared on her face. It was small, but it made all the difference. "It's all right, dear," she said. "Neither have I."

* * *

"Why don't you freshen up? The guest bath's that way." Mrs. Stevens pointed down the hall of her modest but immaculate home before taking a closer look at the filth that covered me from head to toe. "On second thought," she said, "perhaps the laundry room would work better."

"Thanks." I followed her through the dining room, where a table was set with what looked like sterling silver and linen napkins, and down a hallway with tiles so white I was almost afraid to step on them. I was grateful she hadn't sent me to the guest bathroom. Undoubtedly it was adorned with those seashell soaps that have never been placed under running water and guest towels folded in such a way that the one you use looks conspicuously unkempt when you hang it back up.

"Soap's on the counter and towels are under the sink. I'll just be in the kitchen." She disappeared down the hallway, and I stepped into a room redolent of clean clothes and fabric softener. Glancing cautiously toward the sink, I saw that the soap was a plain old bar of Ivory. My kind of place.

As I turned on the faucet and sluiced the dust from my hands and arms, I checked out the room. Not surprisingly, it looked much different from the tiny laundry room in my apartment. For one thing there were no piles of dirty clothes on the floor. For another thing, a sewing machine and neatly organized spools of colored thread sat on a table in an alcove behind me. Several pieces of mending lay in a wicker basket by the table.

I had never been much of a seamstress. Despite Gam's best efforts, all of my experiences ended up with ruined fabric and bloody fingers.

I filled my hands with water and splashed it on my face. Instantly the water running down the drain turned a murky gray. Fumbling under the sink, I found a towel and used it to dry my face and blot at least a cursory layer of grime from my clothes. By the time I was finished with it, the towel had gone from a light blue to a blackish purple. I hid it in the empty washing machine, hoping no one would find it until I was gone.

Stepping out into the hallway, I was met by a heavenly aroma—butter, garlic, cooking sherry, and a dozen other smells I couldn't name. I followed the irresistible scents, trying to keep my tongue in my mouth. As I got closer, I could hear the sound of a knife on a chopping board and Mrs. Stevens humming softly.

"I hope you like Shiitake mushrooms," she said as I entered the kitchen. Now I could smell capers and some kind of nutty spice. In a large wok, a dark brown sauce bubbled enticingly.

"I could eat shoe leather if it smelled like that," I said, meaning every word. That brought another of those little smiles to her lips.

"Well, why don't you finish up this salad and take it into the dining room while I serve." She untied her apron and took two plates from a shelf above her. They looked like the kind of china that had been in the family for years—the kind of plates I usually end up breaking.

"You don't have to get out anything fancy—" I started, but she shushed me with a wave of her hand.

"You were expecting a Whopper maybe? On that waxy paper?"

I shook my head silently, although that was pretty much exactly what I had been planning on for lunch until she came along.

"Well then, finish that salad and I'll dish this up before it burns."

I glanced at the wok again, wondering how she'd managed to whip up something so quickly. I hadn't smelled anything cooking when we came in. She shot me another impatient glance, and I quickly scooped the vegetables she'd been chopping into a glass bowl and carried them to the dining room.

"You sit there," Mrs. Stevens said, following me to the table. She indicated a chair at the end. "That was Mr. Stevens's place before he passed." She laid out two plates and went into the kitchen again.

I gave the embroidered upholstery on the chairs a nervous peek, but needn't have worried. They were all covered in plastic. As I took my seat, Mrs. Stevens returned with a pitcher of water and glasses. "Water cleanses the palate between each bite so that you can more easily appreciate the flavors of the dish."

I could have told her that wasn't going to be a problem for my palate. It was already singing praises of the dish, and I had yet to take a single bite.

She bowed her head and I followed suit. "Oh, Lord," she said, "for this bounty we are about to receive, we are grateful. Let us remember that all good things come from Thee. Let us remember that all good things we do serve Thee. And let my scallywag of a grandson remember that if he doesn't leave on his mission within six months, everything that I've given him will be taken away."

I bit my lip, trying not to giggle until she made it to the end of the prayer.

"Amen," she said.

"Amen," I echoed.

I don't know if she'd planned to talk during the meal. If so, she was sadly disappointed. From the moment the first forkful entered my mouth, I was lost. I have no idea exactly what was in the dish she served, and I am certain I couldn't make it myself, even if red-hot pokers were placed against my feet. But if that dish is not served in heaven, someone needs to speak with the chef.

When, at last, I scraped up the final portion of my food with the edge of my fork and swallowed it with a pang of regret, I realized that Mrs. Stevens was watching me. Her plate looked hardly touched, and I briefly considered asking her if she was going to finish hers.

"Good?" she asked.

"Mmmm-hmmm-hmmm," I moaned gently, rubbing my stomach.

"Well it's good to cook for someone who appreciates their meal." For a moment her face had softened, but as she laid her fork beside her plate, her features drew into a series of harsh planes again. I was so lost in the afterglow of the food, I barely registered the cold calculation returning to her eyes. "Of course, I didn't bring you here just to feed you," she said.

"No?" I was still feeling a little slow and lost. Good food always does that to me.

"No, dear," she said, the words like two sharp little stabs. "You've come back to learn about your grandparents. And I might be the only person in this town willing to tell you the truth."

Now I was wide awake. I sat forward. "You will? You'll tell me?"

"Yes, I will." She cupped her hands in front of her as though trapping a small bird, a hard smile on her face. "But I don't think you'll like what you're going to hear."

CHAPTER TWENTY-SEVEN

As a small girl listening to Gam's stories in the shade of the trees behind her house, I always had little pebbles of cold flesh raise on the backs of my arms when she got to the part where the witch told Hansel to stick out his finger to see whether he was fat enough to eat. It seemed like I was always eating something when Gam came to that scene. I'd stop chewing whatever I had in my mouth and would nervously examine my own fingers, wondering if I were plump enough to be eaten by the wicked witch.

Sitting at the dining room table, I felt myself transported back to those childhood days. Beneath my sweatshirt, goose bumps prickled the tiny hairs on my arms. Helplessly I found myself glancing at my fingers again. The taste of the food—ambrosial before—had gone cold and greasy in my mouth.

"I want to hear it all," I said. "But first I'd like to know why you're telling me this."

She hadn't expected that. Her smile faltered, and her hands briefly squeezed together. If she'd been holding a bird, her bony fingers would have crushed it. She recovered quickly though. "Do I need a reason?" She laughed. "I'm telling you about your grandmother—and your grandfather—because I can and because no one else will."

I nodded. "Fair enough." Even though she hadn't told me the real reason, I could see it in her eyes. Maybe it's a female thing. I've never been good at reading men, but I can tell from a mile away when a woman dislikes another woman. Mrs. Stevens disliked Gam—maybe even hated her.

"Tell me what you know," she said. "There's no point in rehashing what you've already heard."

I told her everything Nan had said, leaving out only my personal reaction to it all. I figured she'd already heard it anyway, and was I curious to see what her response might be. On that count I was disappointed. She managed to hold a poker face through my entire story. I didn't tell her anything about the body I'd found or my suspicions of who the dead man might be.

When I'd finished speaking, she studied me for a moment and then took off her glasses to polish them with her napkin. Looking down while watching me from the corner of her eye, she said, "He *did* come back, you know."

"My grandfather?" I asked, my breath catching in my throat. "How do you know?"

"I saw him."

"You saw my grandfather. *After* he came back?"

"Saw him. Talked to him. Listened to his side of the story."

I stared at her dumbfounded. "*His* side of the story. What do you mean *his* side of the story? Did he claim that he didn't molest my mother? That it was all just a big misunderstanding?" My voice was rising, and I could feel the blood pounding in my temples, but Mrs. Stevens remained calm. If anything, her smile increased a little.

"That's exactly what he claimed."

"And you believed him?" I pushed my plate away, unmindful of the fork that clattered onto the table.

Mrs. Stevens put on her glasses, adjusting them until they fit just so. "Is there any reason I shouldn't have believed him? Any witnesses other than Elsie?"

"What about my mother?" I shot back, trying to get myself under control. "Or do you think she and Gam made it all up?"

Mrs. Stevens—whom I was beginning to picture in a black-pointed hat, handing out candy canes to children—only chuckled. "You see, dear. That's the interesting thing. Your mother never *did* tell her side of the story to anyone. Apparently she was too *trau-ma-tized* by the whole ordeal. Everything happened so quickly, and it was dark."

She watched me, taking obvious delight in my discomfort. Part of me wanted to get up and leave. Obviously she was lying. But another part of me needed to hear her out. There might be some shred of truth in her lies. If there was, I wanted to hear it.

"Your mother never talked to you about it either, did she?" she asked softly. I shook my head.

"Why did he come to *you*?" I asked.

"Why do you think?" For a split second, something crossed her eyes—a flash of emotion too brief to catch—and then it was veiled again. "I was the newspaper editor, of course. He thought I could tell his side."

"And did you?"

She glared at me. "No."

"If you were so sure of his innocence, why not print his story? That's what reporters do—protect the *innocent*." I spat out the last word, my hands clenching and unclenching on the tabletop.

She leaned toward me, her face so close I could see the veins in her head and neck throbbing. "Don't tell me about reporting, girl," she shouted into my face. "I was reporting the news before you were wearing diapers."

"Then why not?" Now I was shouting too.

Abruptly she stood, snatching her plate so that half of her food spilled onto the table. "Your grandmother killed him before I got the chance." Clutching her china in trembling hands, she turned and stumbled into the kitchen.

Frozen in my chair, I stared at the spreading puddle of brown sauce. *It's only an accusation,* I told myself. *An accusation from a woman who obviously has an axe to grind.* And yet hadn't I already come halfway to believing it too?

To be completely honest, I'd come a lot more than halfway to believing that Gam killed my grandfather. Mrs. Stevens, whom I could now hear crying softly in the kitchen, had only articulated the belief I'd been too scared to say out loud. A thought came to me.

Putting both hands on the arms of my chair, afraid that my legs might not hold me, I pushed myself up. In the kitchen Mrs. Stevens leaned over the sink, head bowed.

"Did you love him?" I asked her.

She mumbled something I couldn't understand.

"You loved my grandfather, didn't you? That's why you're making this all up."

She turned around, her eyes red and blazing. Mascara dripped sloppily down her cheeks. "You have no idea what you're talking about."

"Then explain to me how you could stick up for a man who beat his family—who molested his daughter. How could you even think of defending an animal like that?"

She collapsed against the counter, wiping long, black raccoon tracks across her cheeks with the back of one hand.

"You didn't know Stewart. Not many people did." She took a deep breath. "He was a hard man with a quick temper. But that's the way he was raised—spare the rod and spoil the child."

"And that makes it all right?"

She dismissed me with a wave of her hand. "Back then lots of men hit their wives occasionally. Your grandfather was no better or worse than anyone else. Elsie knew he was a hard man when she married him. Pretty little Elsie Sullivan could have had any man in town she wanted, and there were plenty of men interested in her. But she picked Stewart. So who was to blame?"

I bit my tongue, letting her continue.

"After Elsie ran him out of town in '64, there were a lot of wagging tongues. I never believed a word of what they said about Stewart and little Trinity—he wasn't that kind of man. But there was no way he could come back to tell what really happened. Folks would've strung him up before he got the first word out of his mouth. He called me, and I told him so. He tried to call your grandmother, too, but she wouldn't listen."

"But he *did* come back," I said, unable to keep myself from at least accepting that she believed what she was saying.

"Yes." She nodded. "After twenty years he came back. And look what it got him. He came back to her on his hands and knees after all that time. Told me he was bringing something that would change her mind. But he never got the chance, did he? She killed him first."

"If you really believed that, why didn't you contact the police? Or at least put something in the paper. Why wait all these years to tell anyone?"

She shook her head. "You really are a naïve little thing. Do you honestly think I was the only person who knew what she'd done? Everyone in town knew what happened—at least the old-timers. They said he deserved what he got. When Elsie ran, they all said, 'Let's just let bygones be bygones.'"

"But you—"

"I make my living from this town." She waved her hand in front of her. "This house may not seem like much. And to you, my little newspaper probably seems even less. But they're all I have. And the people in this town are the ones who buy the ads that keep my paper afloat. They don't want to hear bad news, and they certainly don't want me speaking ill of a woman they all love. If I'd written your grandfather's story or called the police, they'd have shut me down like *that*." She snapped her fingers—a hollow click.

A cold, dull ache filled my chest as I tried to digest what she was telling me. Surely it wasn't true, and yet . . .

"You asked me if I loved him," she said, her voice barely above a whisper. "In a way, I guess I did. I'd never have left my husband, but I could see the pain written into Stewart's face when he came back. I could feel everything he'd gone through. He wasn't a perfect man, but he deserved better than Elsie gave him. And I didn't have the heart to tell him."

"Tell him what?" I wrapped my arms across my chest, cupping my elbows.

Mrs. Stevens's eyes glittered. She took a deep, steadying breath. "That your grandmother had taken a lover while he was gone."

Her words knocked the air out of me. Suddenly I couldn't seem to inhale. "When?" I gasped. "Who?"

She only shook her head. "I've told you more than enough. Besides," she said, taking obvious pleasure in my reaction, "if you keep on digging, you'll find out for yourself anyway."

CHAPTER TWENTY-EIGHT

Most people go to their therapist with their problems or to their minister. I go to the laundromat. It's much cheaper—a roll of quarters can last through a world of problems—and you can clean your clothes while you clear you conscience.

I love watching the whirl of colored laundry as it's tossed in front of the dryer window. It's like having an aquarium—without the worry of finding your favorite fish floating belly-up in the morning.

"So do you believe her?" I asked a lone white sock as it tumbled past. I shook my head. "I don't want to either, but it does answer a lot of questions."

Not that I believed for a second that my grandfather hadn't molested my mother. That was a stretch on far too many levels. Most importantly, Gam had no reason to lie about it. But the part of the story about Gam killing my grandfather went a long way toward explaining why she had left, and why she never came back. And it dovetailed perfectly with the body I'd found.

"So I guess I can go home now. I can always come back later to ask Nan more about my mom and cad. The police can handle the rest." A flapping pair of jeans gave me a disgusted wave of one leg before disappearing from view.

"*What?* It's not like I haven't learned more than I ever wanted to know about Gam." That line from *A Few Good Men* flashed across my brain. *You want the truth? You can't handle the truth.* "All right, so I'm not as tough as I thought I was. In less than forty-eight hours I find out that my grandfather was a child molester and my grandmother was a murderer. Can you blame me for not wanting to hear any more?"

The buzzer on the dryer gave a teeth-jangling *brrrraaaaappp,* and the orange light went out.

"My thoughts exactly."

With my mind made up, I opened the dryer and dumped my clothes into one of those wheeled carts the laundromat provides. As I started matching up socks, something occurred to me.

If Gam killed Grandpa, who moved his body? The mysterious lover Gam had supposedly taken? At the time, I'd assumed Mrs. Stevens's accusation was just a bitter old woman's last swipe at a rival she'd always been jealous of. But someone had obviously hidden my grandfather's body. Was someone trying to protect Gam even after she was dead?

"But then whose was the body the sheriff found?" I asked a rumpled, white T-shirt. "I'll tell you something," I said, folding the shirt in half and then in half again. "There's more to this story than Mrs. Stevens is letting on. And I'm going to find out what."

Just then, a frumpy-looking woman with badly sunburned legs extending out from a wildly flowered pair of shorts stepped through the doorway and shot me a strange look. Smiling at her, I held up my folded clothes and said, "I'll have you know that I have some very intelligent laundry!"

* * *

By the time I got back to the motel, it was after seven. The rain had stopped a few hours earlier, and although my poor car still smelled musty, at least the upholstery had dried out. I could see several families leaving their rooms—presumably in search of dinner. Not surprisingly, at the thought of dinner my mind began conjuring up images of a thick, juicy burger covered with sautéed onions and hot mustard, next to a pile of greasy fries. Instantly my mouth filled with saliva.

Climbing the stairs, I tried to extract the key from my pants pocket without dropping my laundry. This was easier said than done. I could just picture myself tripping and falling over the railing.

What do you want me to put down for the cause of death, Sheriff?

Severe uncoordination.

Finally I managed to get the key out of my pocket and into the lock. As I turned the handle and pushed the door open, something brushed across the floor. Laying my clothes on the bed, I turned around to see a white rectangle on the dark carpet. Apparently someone had slid a piece of paper under the crack of the door.

Expecting some sort of notice from the motel office, I was surprised to see several lines of hastily scrawled handwriting. The print was tiny and tight, and I had to hold it up to the window to make it out.

The message was brief and to the point, but I read it twice anyway just to make sure it said what I thought it said.

I know about Stewart, the scraggily print read. *I want my share, or I'll go to the police. Meet me at The Stars and Stripes at nine tonight. Come alone, and don't bring your cop friend.*

* * *

According to the motel's night manager, The Stars and Stripes was a bar near the edge of town. Even with his directions, I passed it twice before finding the narrow gravel lot and pulling in. There were roughly a dozen vehicles parked in front of the seedy building—all, except mine, trucks and SUVs.

Getting out of my car, I could hear the steady thump, thump, thump of a jukebox reverberating through the night. As I crunched across the gravel, I checked the windows of the trucks I passed—expecting that at any moment a door would pop open and someone would jump out at me.

As I approached the bar, I tried to peer in the windows. The only thing I could see through the tinted glass was an astonishing variety of neon beer signs. Probably worth a fortune on eBay.

I checked my watch. Almost forty minutes early. Did I really want to do this? I had no idea who had written the note. It could be a psycho, a pervert, a murderer. I considered coming back later, but I knew that if I left now, I'd never work up the nerve to return. "Oh, come on," I said to myself. "You only live once." The sentiment didn't do anything to improve my fears.

If I walked away now, I'd be looking over my shoulder every minute, wondering who might be following me. At least this way I'd be meeting him in a public place. Taking a deep breath, I pushed open the unpainted wooden door and walked in.

Stepping from the outside air into the smoky, alcohol-infused atmosphere of the bar was like walking face-first into the exhaust fumes of a city bus. My eyes began to burn even before the door swung shut behind me. Squinting into the dark haze, I could just make out several small tables spread randomly in front of a mirrored bar. The only bright light in the room was coming from a couple of hooded lamps slung low over two pool tables in the far corner.

The bar was filled with the sounds of men's voices—raucous laughter and animated conversations—but the words were drowned out by the sound of country music so loud it physically assaulted your eardrums. As I stood just inside the doorway, waiting for my eyes to adjust, a skinny man with a handlebar mustache waved a bottle in my direction.

"Hey, schweetheart," he slurred. "What'd it take to get you to come sit on my lap?"

"Whatever it is, you don't have it." Turning my back on the laughter of the men sitting with him, I went in search of an empty table. Near the bar I found a booth that looked like it might have been wiped down sometime in the last decade and gingerly took a seat.

A few minutes later, a peroxide blonde in a skirt that looked three sizes too small squeezed up to my table. She gave me an appraising look. "You lost, darling?"

"I'm meeting someone," I said, straining to be heard over the music.

She nodded sagely and leaned her head toward me in conspiratorial fashion. "Take my advice. Make sure you get a gander at him under the streetlight outside before taking him home. The lights in here can be mighty deceiving."

"I'll keep that in mind."

She grinned as though she'd just earned a twenty-five percent tip. "So, what can I getcha?"

I glanced around for a menu, but the closest thing I could find was a chalkboard offering buy-one-get-one-free black Russians. "You don't have anything to *eat,* do you?"

"Sure." She tapped a red-lacquered fingernail against the tabletop. Seeing my confusion, she took a damp cloth from her serving tray and began to scrub. Slowly the greasy surface cleared enough to reveal a rectangular card under the plastic covering.

If it ain't fried, the card read, we don't have it. That, at least, was a motto I could get behind.

"I'll have the pastrami burger," I said after a minute. "And a side of jalapeno poppers."

"Sure thing." She laboriously inscribed my order onto her pad. "Anything to drink?"

"Do you have Sprite?"

"Sure do," she said. And then with a wink, added, "Stay sober. Getting drunk's how I ended up with my second husband." Sage advice.

Before she could walk away, I touched her wrist and asked, "You haven't heard a man asking around for a woman, have you?"

"Doll," she said, "they all are."

Twenty-five minutes and several drunken propositions later, she was back with my food. I was half sure I'd end up with botulism, but after the first bite, I knew that at least I'd die with a smile on my face.

I'd been watching the door since I'd come in. Several people had entered and left, but none that I recognized. Not that I'd necessarily recognize the note's author. Still, I thought I'd know him when I saw him.

At a few minutes after nine, the door swung open and a man stepped into the bar. He was wearing an overcoat. A baseball cap shadowed his face. He stopped just inside the door and surveyed the room. I tensed as he looked in my direction.

As he began to walk across the room toward me, he reached into the pocket of his coat and pulled out a lighter. He was only a few feet away from me now, but I still couldn't make out his features beneath the shadow of the cap. Tucking a cigarette between his lips, he raised his lighter and flicked the wheel.

The flame from the lighter illuminated his face. It was a face I'd seen before. The kind of face nightmares are made of.

The man standing in front of me was the man with the metallic blue eyes who'd sat beside me at breakfast that morning.

CHAPTER TWENTY-NINE

"Knew you'd show." He surveyed the room—assuring himself I'd come alone—and slid onto the bench across from me. He took a deep drag on his cigarette. The tip glowed brightly as he inhaled, illuminating his face. He looked even creepier in the dim light of the bar than he had that morning.

"Unless you give me a good reason to stay in the next two minutes, I'm out of here," I said, trying to keep the shakiness I felt out of my voice.

His upper lip rose, revealing badly stained brown teeth. A stream of smoke exited his thin nose like stinking dragon's breath before floating lazily up toward the ceiling. "You ain't goin' anywhere, girlie," he drawled.

I stood, but before I could take a step, his hand darted across the table and closed around my wrist. For a moment our eyes locked, and then I pulled my gaze away to take in the other men in the bar. "Sure are a lot of cowboys out there," I said softly. "What do you imagine they'd do if I screamed right now?"

I could feel his fingers tighten—pressing the bones of my wrist together to demonstrate the pain he could cause me if he wanted to—then, all at once he let go. "Sit down for a minute," he said. "I'm not gonna hurtcha."

"Not until I know who you are and what you want."

He took another long drag on his cigarette before tapping the ash into a tin tray on the table. "I'm a friend of your grandfather's. That's all you need to know 'bout who I am. And I'm here to get the money he owes me."

I sat down. "My grandfather's dead."

He laughed—the sound parched and reedy, like a snake slithering through dry grass. "Shoot, I know that, girlie. Why else'd I be talking to you?"

"So you expect me to pay off some gambling debt he supposedly owes you? Or did he stiff you on a bar tab?" My voice was rising. Two men at the next table over stopped their conversation briefly, turning in our direction.

The man who claimed to know my grandfather studied me silently for nearly a minute. His eyes were bright and predatory. At last, he stubbed out his half-smoked cigarette and laid both hands flat on the table. His tan fingers were bone thin, but the knuckles were thick and knobby.

"I ain't here 'bout no bar tab," he said slowly. "Your grandfather was more than just a friend. He was what you might call an associate."

Knowing I was going to regret it, but unable to stop myself, I asked, "An associate in what?"

Instead of answering, he reached into his pocket and pulled out a folded newspaper clipping. Apparently it was my day for newspapers. He pushed the yellowed print across the table to me and watched while I opened it.

The story was dated February 14, 1984. The headline read, Masked Men Pull Off Daring Bank Heist.

Monday morning two masked men robbed the First Central Credit Union at 224 East 27th

South, just hours before its grand opening. According to Detective Ransom Harding of the Salt Lake City Police Department, "At this point the robbery appears to be an inside job. We believe that the criminals made use of a security flaw apparently slipped in during the credit union's recent construction."

Credit union employees found two masked gunmen waiting for them as they entered the building yesterday morning. Employees were forced to open the vault and hand over bags of cash. Although the actual amount taken was not disclosed, sources indicate that a large amount of cash was on hand for the expected busy first day.

Police are questioning Latham Construction, the building contractor, and are said to be searching for Richard Anderson and Myron Snelling, two Latham employees no longer with the firm.

I dropped the paper onto the table, remembering the picture I'd seen of my grandfather standing in front of Echo Lake's newly constructed Zions Bank building. "Which one was he?" I asked without looking up.

"Myron. Always thought that name sounded kind of lame, but he liked it."

"And that would make you Anderson."

"I've been called worse." He drummed his fingers on the tabletop. "Do you want to know why he did it? I thought it was a very touching story when he told me. Very touching."

I shook my head. Mrs. Stevens said that my grandfather was bringing something back to change Gam's mind. "I think I've got that part figured out."

He nodded, watching me with an anticipatory gleam in his eyes.

"What do you expect me to do about this?" I asked. "If you're trying to blackmail me, it won't work."

He laughed his thin, papery chuckle again. The sound of it rattled my nerves. "I could care less 'bout the old man," he said. "I just want my share of the money. We was supposed to split it, but he disappeared."

"And you think I have it?" The thought was so ludicrous, I couldn't help laughing.

The effect of my laughter was immediate. The man's face tightened, his already stretched skin looking as though it might tear at any moment. His lips pulled back into a snarl. "I've waited a long time," he growled. "Either you got the money or it's still in the house."

On the table, the fingers of his right hand slid apart to reveal a glittering silver blade. "Either way, I don't get my share, someone's gonna end up dead."

Suddenly I remembered the second body. "It was you, wasn't it? You killed that man in my grandmother's house." His cold eyes didn't flinch.

I pushed the article back across to him. "If you think the money's in the house, why not get it yourself?" I could no longer keep the fear out of my voice. Room full of people or not, I had no doubt this man was willing to kill me right then and there.

His fingers closed, the knife vanishing beneath them. "Cops are all over that place. I can't get anywhere near it.

And some psycho just 'bout took my head off when I tried to get a closer look last night."

Some psycho? What was he talking about? "How do you know the money's even there?" I asked. "Maybe he spent it or hid it somewhere else."

"No." His hands disappeared into his coat pockets and with them the knife. He pulled out another cigarette, lit it, and tucked it between his lips, where it moved as he spoke. "That old guy gave me the slip twenty years ago. He took the money, but the way I hear it, he didn't live long enough to spend it. I hear his old lady did him in soon as he got back."

"Where did you hear that?" I asked, my hands balling into fists.

He grinned, his tobacco-stained teeth like chips of walnut shell. "I keep my ear to the ground."

"But why now? Why wait twenty years to come for it if you're so sure the money's still there?"

"Didn't know where he lived—didn't even know his real name—till I seen the picture of him and your grandmother in the paper."

"Gam's obituary."

He nodded. "Yeah, that was it. I seen that picture, and I knew it was him. Recognized that ugly puss right away."

"I can't help you," I said. "I can't get into the house either. The police have it sealed off. And even if I could, I have no idea where the money would be. Someone probably found it years ago."

Instantly he was across the table, the glowing ember of his cigarette only inches from my eyes. Somehow the knife was back in his hand, its tip pressed against my chest. "You got two days," he whispered, his breath like rotten meat.

"I'm watching you, and I wanna see you in that house tomorrow. And don't go to the cops or you're dead."

Before I could say a word, he faded into the crowd and walked out the door.

CHAPTER THIRTY

The entire drive back to the motel I kept my eyes glued to the rearview mirror, convinced each new set of headlights that appeared there was following me. I ran across the parking lot and up the stairs with the staccato lub-dub-dub, lub-dub-dub of my heart pounding in my ears. Not until I turned the deadbolt and checked the window lock twice did I feel even remotely secure.

The red message light on my phone was blinking, and my first thought was of Anderson. With trembling fingers, I punched in the two-digit code. A computerized voice said, "You have one new message."

Bracing myself to hear the cold, threatening voice, I played the message. "Hi, Shandra. This is Clay . . . at the sheriff's office." I smiled—half in relief, and half at his assumption that I might not know which Clay it was. "I just wanted to check up on you, see how you're doing. No more dead bodies, I hope." I thought about the knife Anderson had placed at my chest, and my smile disappeared.

"I was also wondering . . ." he continued. "If you're not doing anything tomorrow night, maybe I could take you out to dinner and then horseback riding? Call me in the morning."

A beep, and then the compu-voice said, "No new messages."

Still gripping the receiver, I stared at the phone. *Call him,* a voice in my head demanded. *Call him right now and tell him everything that's going on.* But I could hear another voice as well—*Don't go to the cops or you're dead.*

"To hear saved messages, press—" Carefully I set the receiver back in its cradle and collapsed onto the bed. My brain felt sick and muddled, as though I'd been out in the sun too long. Lying onto the pillow, I wiped a hand across my brow. My palm came away damp with perspiration.

"Just give me a little time," I said—not sure which voice I was answering. "I just need to rest. In the morning I'll—"

Whatever I was going to do in the morning evaporated from my mind as I escaped into sleep.

* * *

The sound of my cell phone pulled me from a confused and unsatisfying sleep. Untangling myself from the blankets, I sat halfway up and fumbled for the talk button.

"Hello?" I mumbled, my mouth dry and cottony.

"Some friend you are." The voice on the other end of the line sounded both irate and amused, but it was as welcome as a down comforter.

"Bobby!"

"So you do remember me," he sulked. "I only manage to get you freed from jail by the best attorney in Salt Lake—at no charge, I might add—and you don't even bother to call and thank me."

"It's so good to hear from you," I said, rubbing my eyes.

"Yeah, yeah. I'll bet you say that to all the men who spring you from the gray bar motel." Now his tone was all amusement. He was having fun at my expense. But I knew I deserved it.

"Only to the handsome ones," I said in the smokiest voice I could muster first thing in the morning.

"Don't forget smart," he added. "And a great dancer."

Flirting with Bobby was safe. As a couple of "overage" single Mormons, we both knew what the dating scene was like in Utah, and we'd made a pact together. Not the if-we're-both-single-and-thirty-five-we'll-marry-each-other kind of pact. Just the opposite. No matter how old we got, we would *never* date each other.

I kind of liked the idea of a doddering old woman telling a prune of a man, "How about asking out that lady on the park bench. She looks peaceful."

And him answering, "I think she's dead."

"I'm sorry," I said. "I really did mean to call. Things have just been a little crazy up here." Daylight was streaming around the edges of the thick curtains. Turning to the digital clock, I saw that it was nearly nine.

"Why *are* you still there?" The laughter disappeared from Bobby's voice. "Get back home and let the local cops deal with that stuff."

The thought of holing up in my own cozy apartment and getting back to work was an attractive one. But I couldn't leave yet.

"If this is about the murder," Bobby said, "you don't need to worry. They identified the body this morning, and there's no connection to you."

"They did?" Now I was wide awake.

"Yeah it's a retired cop. Nobody knows what he was doing at Echo Lake, but—"

"Ransom Harding," I interrupted, remembering the detective from the newspaper article. "Was that his name?"

There was silence on the other end of the line for several seconds, and when Bobby spoke again, his voice was cautious. "How could you know that?"

I'd barely managed to kick off my shoes before falling asleep. Now I toed my feet back into them. "Bobby, I need you to do me a favor."

"Shandra, whatever you're into up there, you have to let the police handle it. You're a reporter, not a cop."

Under other circumstances I would have given him a stern lecture about the relationships between law enforcement and the media, but I didn't have time for it this morning.

"Listen, Bobby," I dropped my voice, remembering how thin the walls were, "I'll go to the cops soon enough, but there's something I have to check on first." I spoke quickly, not letting him interrupt. "There was a bank robbery in February 1984. First-something credit union. Ransom Harding was the lead detective. See what you can get on the case."

"What's this all about?" I could almost hear Bobby's eyes twitching.

"Just see what you can find out," I said, grabbing my keys and heading for the door. "I think my grandfather may have been involved, and I might know where the money is. Oh, and also, I think his partner may have murdered Detective Harding."

I hung up before Bobby could tell me again not to get involved and switched off my phone for good measure. If he complained later, I'd tell him I lost service.

CHAPTER THIRTY-ONE

By the time I reached Gam's house, the last of the morning overcast had burned away, leaving the air warm and still. I stopped in the road, letting my car's engine run, and mulled over my options. I knew I should go to the police, and I would go no matter what I found in the house. If the money *was* there, I'd give that to the police as well.

It wasn't the money that was driving me, nor the threat. Talking to Bobby, I'd realized that everything revolved around the house. Gam had fled from it. My grandfather had been killed in it, as had been Ransom Harding. Pete had warned me away from it. The man at the bar thought money was hidden in it, and if he could be believed, someone had driven him away from it.

It was as though Gam's house was calling to me—tempting me with the answers to whatever was happening here. And just maybe with some answers about myself as well.

My decision made, I pulled several hundred feet up the road, until I found a flat, brushy area just wide enough to hide my car. If Clay came cruising by again, I didn't want him to realize that I was inside.

I pulled as far in as I could. "Sorry," I whispered to Royce, as branches squealed along his hood and doors, "I promise I'll get you a new paint job when this is all over." He knew I was lying—I could barely afford new oil—but he drove in anyway. From the side of the road, I could still see a little of his red paint and a flash of chrome, but only if I was looking for them.

Returning to the house, I walked down the center of the cracked asphalt road, leaving plenty of room between the woods on either side of me. Anderson had said something about a psycho attacking him when he tried to get into the house. That could have been the man I'd seen in the woods.

I stopped several yards short of the porch, staring into the trees, and waited for some sign of movement. If someone wanted to keep me out of the house, this was his chance to do it. The only sound was the rat-a-tat of a woodpecker, the only movement a pair of squirrels chasing one another through the treetops. After several minutes, I took a deep breath, ducked under the crime scene tape, and climbed the porch steps.

The interior of Gam's house was pretty much as I remembered it, except for the dozens of footprints now covering the floor. It was obvious the sheriff had gone out of his way not to step on my tracks or those of the late Detective Harding. The book on the coffee table was gone. Evidence?

What was I waiting for? A boogeyman to jump out at me? Gam's spirit to whisper advice? I felt certain the house was empty, and yet a heavy sense of oppression seemed to squeeze in on me with every breath I took. If Gam had felt this as well, I could understand why she had left. No matter what I found, this was the last time I would come in. I'd rather pay someone to move Gam's things than feel the sorrow and pain that seeped out of the very walls around me.

Climbing the stairs, I told myself someone might be up there, all the while knowing that no one was. This time everything was calm. No bodies lying on the floor. No shock at seeing myself in Gam's mirror. A dust-free rectangle on Gam's dresser marked the spot where the music box had been. I imagined they'd taken that for evidence as well.

The obvious place to start looking was the closet where I'd found my grandfather's body. I assumed that the sheriff had already searched the room, but he was looking for a murder weapon, not the proceeds of a bank robbery.

Carefully stepping over the dark stain on the floor, I entered the closet. Another memory from my childhood bubbled to the surface. As a little girl I used to burrow my way through Gam's outfits, pretending I was a jungle explorer. The cachet of her perfume would fill my nostrils as the textures of each fabric brushed against my cheeks.

Now as my eyes adjusted to the darkness, I could see that moths had gotten to all of her outfits. I started with the boxes and bags on the top shelf. What I found was more old clothing—hats, shoes with broken heels, a tattered grocery bag containing a dozen of my grandfather's ties—the detritus of daily life that collect over time.

The rest of the closet was of no more help—a box of tax papers, a stack of *National Geographic*s. Feeling like a snoop, I quickly sifted through Gam's dresser drawers. Nothing there either. Under the bed was a promising box. But when I opened it, I found ancient rolls of gift wrap and bows.

I tried tapping on a couple of the walls, looking for secret compartments like they do in the movies, but the idea of Gam stashing a bag full of money in a hidden cache was so

ludicrous that I quickly stopped. My mother's old room—
the room I'd slept in as a girl—was next. The closet there
looked much more interesting. It was narrow but deep and
filled with stacks of old boxes.

Propping open the door to get more light, I tried the first
carton and immediately forgot all about murders and bank
robberies. Piled nearly to the top of the cardboard flaps, in
no discernable order, were hundreds of photos I'd never seen
before.

I thought that a tiny girl in a frilly white dress was my
mother. Another showed Gam and my grandfather standing
beside a 1950s sedan with a couple I didn't recognize.
Moving slowly from photo to photo, I studied the faces
looking back at me and wondered who they were and how
they had known my family.

Running my fingers over the glossy surfaces, a deep
feeling of sadness—almost despair—washed over me. Until
I'd returned to Echo Lake, I'd felt no special loss at my lack
of familial ties. How can you miss something you've never
had? But looking at these people, I discovered a huge empti-
ness inside myself.

I desperately wanted someone sitting beside me, pointing
at the faces and naming them. I wanted someone to tell me
the stories behind each photograph—to laugh at long-lost
memories and share them with me. My brother and I seldom
spoke to each other—and when we did, it was about
mundane things, safe things—so I had no idea if he'd ever
felt this way. For his sake, I hoped not.

I let the pictures slip from my fingers into the box, realizing that for the most part they belonged to a world I'd
never know. In another box I discovered a gorgeous, mint-

green satin gown that must have been from my mother's prom. I whispered my fingers over the shiny fabric, trying to imagine how she must have looked in it. I wished I'd been able to wear it to my own prom.

I was flipping through a stack of my mother's school papers when I realized how hot and stuffy the closet had become. Sweat ran down the sides of my temples, and breathing was an effort. I'd spent enough time in there to know I wasn't going to find a bag of money or the answers to any of my questions. My hands looked like I'd spent the last hour petting dust bunnies. There was nothing to wipe them off on since the rest of me was just as bad. I pushed the boxes back where they belonged.

Looking toward the front of the closet, I saw that the light in the bedroom had taken on a strange grainy quality, as though it was filled with dust. As I walked to the door, I suddenly realized I could smell smoke. Something was on fire! I stumbled out into the room and began to cough. A thin, gray mist swirled near the ceiling.

I pulled open the bedroom door. Instantly thick, black smoke billowed into the room. Somewhere below I could hear the crackling of flames. Gagging, I pushed the door shut and rushed to the window. I turned the latch and shoved up on the frame, but it wouldn't budge. I pushed harder and my hand slipped, driving splinters of wood into my palm. Wincing at the pain, I turned to see greasy tendrils reaching in under the door.

The only way out was to break the glass. I searched the room for something to use as a hammer, but the gray haze made it almost impossible to see. I pulled a blanket from the bed, balled it around my hand, and my fist slammed against the window. Nothing. The acrid air burned my lungs. Tossing aside the blanket, I tried again—harder. This time a crack appeared in the bottom pane. I could feel myself growing dizzy.

Closing my eyes, I raised my fist over my shoulder and slammed it against the window with all my strength. The glass shattered and my arm went through. A burst of white-hot pain shot up my arm. I opened my eyes and saw a shard of glass imbedded in the flesh between my wrist and elbow. Bright red blood oozed from the wound and dripped down my wrist as I pulled the glass loose, but there was no time to worry about that now. I had to get out.

Sucking up the fresh outside air, I used the blanket to knock the remaining glass away. Smoke poured out from behind me. I could feel the floor growing warm beneath my feet. I swung one leg over the frame, and for a minute everything went gray. I clung to the windowsill, trying to keep from fainting, and ducked my head through the opening. It was less than fifteen feet to the ground. Even if I fell out, the grass would cushion my fall.

I was leaning out, preparing to let myself drop, when the propane tank outside exploded. A wall of super-heated air, like a fiery hand, pushed me back into the window and I stumbled across the room.

I must have blacked out for a second, because when I opened my eyes again, I was lying sprawled on the floor. Although intense heat baked my face, I could barely see the flames for the thick smoke. Embers floated across the room and landed on the backs of my arms. I could feel them burning my skin, but deciding what to do about it seemed beyond me.

The window had disappeared and smoke continued to roil beneath the door. Water poured from my eyes as I stared dazedly around the room. There was no way out. I was going to die in here. The thought crossed my mind that I wouldn't be the first one.

Somehow, I managed to crawl to the door. The knob was hot beneath my fingers, but I held on and pulled. Cowering against the floor, I scooted out into the hallway. Swirling blackness obliterated everything. With a vague idea of making it into Gam's room I dragged myself forward. Even with my face pressed against the floor, each breath tore like ragged claws at my throat and caught in my lungs. Dark images floated in front of my eyes and disappeared.

I must have lost my direction, because as I reached forward with my right hand, the floor disappeared beneath my fingers and I dropped forward. My chin slammed against the corner of a step, and I went cartwheeling down the stairs. A burst of stars exploded in front of my eyes as my head collided with the wall. A piercing sound filled my ears, and it was only when I hit the landing at the bottom, knocking the air out myself, that I realized it was the sound of my own screaming.

Somewhere nearby, a beam collapsed with a roar and a burst of hot red sparks. I couldn't go any farther. My ears were ringing, and I could feel consciousness disappearing. When I tried to crawl forward my arms refused to obey. I thought I could hear someone calling my name.

I raised my head, but the darkness was so complete, I couldn't tell if my eyes were open or not. Arms closed around me, and I passed out.

CHAPTER THIRTY-TWO

The rest of the morning was a blurred collage, patched together from a few brief moments when I was fairly sure I was awake and a stream of strange, constantly changing images. I vaguely remembered throwing up on someone—a fireman, maybe?—trying to apologize and feeling like my throat was tearing itself apart as I coughed and retched some more.

Later a woman gave me a glass of water to drink and rubbed something on my arms and neck that burned at first and then turned pleasantly cool. In the middle of it all, I thought I heard a man's voice speaking softly to me while his fingers brushed back my hair. Of course, that last part was probably my imagination.

When I finally came to, I was lying on a hospital bed in a brightly lit room. A short man wearing glasses and a long, white coat was reading what I assumed to be my chart.

"You're awake," he said, noting something on the clipboard with a ballpoint pen.

"Am I?" My mouth felt sore and grainy, like I'd been gargling with sand, and my thoughts seemed to be making their way through Jell-O. "I feel kind of loopy," I said.

"It's the drugs." As he leaned over my bed, I read his nametag, *Dr. Tae*. He slid a stethoscope, fresh out of the refrigerator, down the front of my hospital gown, and it was all I could do to keep from pulling his arm from its socket.

"Sorry," he said, "that's probably a little cold."

Just my luck to get Captain Obvious for a doctor. "Am I going to live?" I asked, trying to sit up.

He pushed a button that raised the top half of my bed. "You're going to be fine as long as you stay out of any more burning houses."

At his words, the reality of what had happened struck my stomach like a cannonball. Dr. Tae must have noticed the look on my face, because he quickly placed a hand on my shoulder. "You're a very lucky woman, Miss Covington."

"I don't feel lucky," I said. What I felt was tired and sore and homesick. My right arm was bandaged from wrist to elbow in white gauze, and my left arm was covered with tiny red burns. My head was pounding like someone had used it to try out their new nine iron, and I could barely swallow.

"But you *are* lucky." His brown eyes were large and serious behind the magnifying lenses of his glasses. "If you hadn't gotten out when you did . . ." He closed his eyes for a moment and shook his head slowly.

As I realized what he was saying, my self-pity disappeared. What was I thinking? Of course I was lucky. I was sulking over a few bumps and bruises when I could have been dead. But how had I gotten out of the house? The last thing I remembered was rolling down the stairs.

"How did I . . ." I began to ask Dr. Tae, before remembering the arms I'd felt closing around me.

"Who?" I said. "Who pulled me from the fire?"

His eyes darted to the right, and for the first time I realized we weren't alone in the room.

* * *

"Hey," Clay said, smiling sheepishly. He was sitting in the corner off to my left in one of those uncomfortable plastic chairs they always had outside the principal's office when I was a kid. A magazine of some kind was folded in his lap.

"It was *you?*" I asked. "You rescued me?"

He scratched his head, looking pleased and embarrassed at the same time.

"But how did you find me?"

"I saw the fire and just went in. You pretty much stumbled into me."

My face heated up as though I were back in the fire. "You . . . saved my life." The words are just cliché until you say them yourself. But he *had.* He'd actually saved my life while risking his own.

"You didn't expect me to leave you in there, did you?" Now he definitely looked embarrassed.

"No. I mean, I guess not. But how did you even know I was there? I hid . . ." I stopped, realizing that *he* was who I'd been hiding from.

". . . your car," he finished for me. "It took almost an hour after the fire to find where you'd stashed it."

He shook his head with a rueful grin. "It was a lucky thing your friend Bobby called, or I'd never have had any idea you were there. It's really him you should be thanking, you know."

Talk about feeling dumb. I could feel my face going scarlet. "I know I shouldn't have gone in there," I said. "I'm sure I broke about twenty laws."

Clay laughed, raising the front legs of his chair off the ground and tilting it back toward the wall. "I'm just glad you're okay. And don't worry about the sheriff. He's still smarting over the way your lawyer took him to town. I'm sure he's not going to give you any flak."

Suddenly I remembered why I'd gone to the house in the first place. "Clay," I said, sitting all the way up. "There's a man here in town. I think he's the one who murdered Ransom Harding. He said he was coming after me next."

"Easy, Shandra." The chair dropped back onto all four legs as Clay stood up. His fingers closed around the magazine.

I looked to the door, my hands shaking, as I wondered whether the murderer might be lurking out in the hallway even as we spoke. "He said he'd kill me if I didn't find his money. He said if I went to the police—"

"It's okay. We've got him."

"He has a knife and he's—"As the meaning of Clay's words finally penetrated my brain, I stopped and looked at him. "You got him?"

Clay's right fist was clenched tightly around the rolled magazine. He put his left hand on my trembling arm. "We found him hanging around outside your motel room. After we found his note in your car, the owner of the Stars and Stripes IDed him as the guy you were with last night. His real name is Reggie Torrance. He's locked up now. He can't hurt you."

"But . . . " For a moment my muddled brain seemed incapable of putting everything together. Then the pieces dropped into place. "Bobby?"

Clay nodded. "You know, if you'd told just told us everything in the first place, we could've helped you."

"Yeah." I swallowed, my throat like sandpaper. "I guess I just wasn't sure who I could trust. I'm sorry."

Clay studied me for long moment, his eyes unreadable. "Do you trust me now?"

"How can I not trust the man who would run into a burning house to rescue me?" I said, my palms strangely damp.

Clay grinned. "Shucks, ma'am, all in a day's work."

But his smile faded away as his fingers tightened on the magazine. "Your grandmother's house . . ."

My breath caught. I was sure I knew the answer, but I had to ask anyway. "Were they . . . able to save . . . *anything?*"

His eyes looked away, but his head gave a quick shake. "No, it burned to the ground."

I reached up and closed my hand around his, my fingers like ice against the warmth of his skin. "I need to see it one last time. Will you take me, please?"

CHAPTER THIRTY-THREE

I don't know what I was thinking as I stared at the charred remains of my grandmother's house. Sometimes when things reach a certain point, rational thought is no longer possible. You feel your mind thrumming like a sparking power line in a high wind. Then, before it completely snaps, it just disengages, leaving you adrift in a sea of nothingness.

I like to believe it's God's built-in circuit breaker.

Sitting in the passenger's seat of Clay's patrol car that smelled faintly of vomit and less faintly of cheap aftershave, I wasn't thinking about everything I'd lost—the pictures, the clothes, the mementos. I wasn't thinking about the irony that only a few days earlier I didn't even know those things existed. I wasn't thinking about how the only links to my past—fragile as they were—had disappeared.

I wasn't thinking at all.

"Are you okay?" Clay's voice floated to me from far away, from another continent maybe. I tried to look at him but couldn't seem to pull my eyes from the gutted frame.

"Maybe we should go."

"No. I . . . don't want . . . to leave." It took every ounce of strength I had to get the words out. The tendons in my throat creaked like rusty hinges.

"Sure, all right." He cleared his throat. "I just thought it might be easier if you didn't have to, you know, see."

Something in his voice pulled me partway out of my stupor. In the few days we'd known each other, he'd gone from being a cop to a friend. I don't make friends easily or quickly, but somehow he was an exception. I turned toward him, noticing the concern in his eyes, the worry lines bracketing his mouth.

"I don't . . ." I felt heat rising in my throat and fought to keep it back. I wasn't going to cry. I hate crying worse than almost anything.

Clay leaned across the seat and put a hand on my shoulder. "Is there anything I can do?"

I shook my head, not trusting myself to speak. I wasn't going to bawl. Not now. Not in front of him. Everything began to go a blurry gray.

"It's okay to cry," he said, brushing his fingers across my cheek.

"No, I can't," I said, the words hitching in my throat. I scrubbed the backs of my hands across my eyes, but it only made matters worse.

"Why not?" The worry in his eyes was now unmistakable, the anxiousness so real I could almost touch it.

Without warning everything crashed down on me, the reality of the last four days a tidal wave I could neither avoid nor resist. I buried my head in my arms, tears dripping down my cheeks, soaking the sleeves of my sweatshirt. "I can't cry," I sobbed. "Because if I start, I don't think I'll be able to stop."

* * *

I hate crying. The way your nose gets all red and stuffy. How your face feels stretched too tight, like a poorly fitting mask. Your voice sounds nasally and hoarse. It always makes me feel like a little kid who doesn't want to leave the amusement park. It makes me feel about eight years old.

The only thing I hate worse than crying, is crying in front of anyone else.

"Are you okay?" Clay asked.

"Just give me a minute," I said more sharply than I meant to. We were standing outside his patrol car, a couple hundred feet from the crumbled remains of Gam's house. I had turned away from him and the house, trying to regain some semblance of control. A couple of firemen poking through ashes glanced in my direction.

I wiped an arm across my face, leaving long, black smears on the sleeve of my shirt. So much for run-free mascara.

"Tissue?" Clay held out a folded fast-food napkin.

"Thanks." I took it without turning around and scrubbed at my face. Finding a clean spot on the napkin, I tried to blow my nose discreetly. It didn't work. I sounded like an African elephant with a bad head cold. I was sure the firemen heard it all the way over at the house.

"I'm fine now."

"Do you want to look around?" Clay asked. "Maybe some of your grandmother's things survived."

I glanced toward the smoking pile. It didn't look hopeful. Still, it wasn't like I had anywhere else to go. "Sure," I said. "And thanks for the napkin."

"No problem. Just wish I had a real box of tissues or a handkerchief."

We walked up the hill, past where I'd parked my car the day I arrived. The grass that had been so long and green was wilted and shriveled from the heat of the blaze. A black film coated everything, and the air was filled with the stink of ashes.

Clay approached the firefighter who seemed to be in charge of things. "Any idea how it started?"

"Hard to say." The man looked to be in his late fifties. Like everything else, his skin was a grimy gray. Even his teeth looked like he'd been chewing on charcoal briquettes. "By the time we got to it, the place was pretty much history," he said. "Old wood like that goes up in a hurry. It may have started in the cellar."

"Cellar?" For the first time, I noticed the pit where the newer section of Gam's house had been. I didn't even know Gam's house had a cellar.

"Yep. Hot water heater and furnace were down there." He turned to Clay. "You think the guy you've got in lock up might've started this?"

"Don't see why he would," Clay said. "Especially if he thought his money was in it. Heck of a coincidence, though."

"Sure is." They shared a look.

The fireman looked at the bandage on my arm. "You're a very lucky lady."

"I keep hearing that," I said, trying to remind myself that he was right.

Using the long metal bar he was holding, he pointed at a blackened chunk of twisted metal about eight feet long. "Propane tank had never been emptied. Figure it was at least a quarter full. When it blew, shrapnel flew everywhere."

I shuddered, remembering how close I'd come to being right next to it when it had exploded. Noticing something shiny amidst the rubble, I started toward it.

"Easy." The fire chief grabbed my shoulder. "There's still hot spots out there. You could melt those tennis shoes right off your feet." He stepped carefully over a blackened beam and retrieved the item I'd seen.

"Looks like some kind of picture frame," he said, handing it to me.

The metal was warm beneath my fingers. Though the silver had warped and run in places, it was still recognizable. The photograph in it was nothing but ashes.

A single fugitive tear slipped down my cheek, and I brushed it away. I held the frame pressed tightly to my chest knowing it might be the only thing left.

"Hey, chief, we got something over here." It was one of the men who'd been poking through the ashes. He was standing halfway down the pit where the fire apparently had started.

"What is it?" The chief called, starting over. Clay and I followed him around the corner of the foundation.

"Look at this!" the man shouted, nearly jumping out of the pit. He leaned back over the hole, moving something with the blade of his axe, and cursed softly.

"It's a body!"

CHAPTER THIRTY-FOUR

"Look like a male to you?"

"Yeah. But it's been here a long time."

"Years, if you ask me—look at the hands."

"Water heater must have tipped over and protected it from most of the . . ."

I tried to pay attention, but I already knew whose body it was and I had no desire to see it again. Walking to where the grass was still tall and green, I stopped beneath the cool shade of a big Douglas fir and sat down next to it. I leaned back and rested my head against the rough bark of its trunk. In the distance I could just make out the warble of a police siren—probably the sheriff. I tuned that out too, letting my mind float along with the whir of insects flitting from one stalk of grass to another.

The smell of pinesap was sweet in my nostrils and the needle-covered ground made a perfect seat. Relishing the cool of the early afternoon breeze on my face, I closed my eyes, giving my physically and emotionally drained body a rest. When the medical examiner arrived, I woke briefly then drifted off again after realizing no one was headed in my direction. I probably would have slept for another hour or more if it hadn't been for the sudden feeling that someone was watching me.

Assuming it was Clay, I squinted my eyes halfway open against the setting sun. Clay and the others were standing around their cars talking. Without getting up, I craned my neck, trying to figure what had awakened me. The breeze had died away, and the grass stood perfectly still. Turning my head, I scanned the woods. Nothing was out of the ordinary, trees dappled with evening light, pinecones, fallen branches.

Then I spotted something almost invisible in a stand of aspen. I stared at the dark shape, trying to be sure of what I was seeing. It could have been a trick of the shadows, and yet I could swear that a man's face was peeking around at me from behind one of the tree trunks. I watched, waiting to see if he moved, but if it was a man, he remained perfectly still.

Planting my hands on the ground, ready to jump to my feet at the first provocation, I stared into the trees. It was a man—I was almost sure of that—and yet I sensed nothing threatening in his demeanor, only—

"Good rest?" I jumped to my feet at the sound of Clay's voice, and he caught me gently around the waist.

"Sorry, I didn't mean to scare you," Clay said. His fingers loosened but didn't entirely leave my sides.

I rested my injured hand on his upper arm, surprised at how comfortable I felt standing this close to him. It wasn't like me. "I guess I was just zoning."

Even before I turned to look into the trees, I knew that the figure would be gone. Still I peered into the shadows. Following my gaze, Clay studied the woods along with me.

"Anything wrong," he asked?

"No," I said, seeing nothing out of the ordinary. "At least, I don't think so."

* * *

As we pulled away from the ruins of Gam's house, Clay turned right, up the hill, instead of toward town. I glanced curiously at him, but he wouldn't catch my eye. Finally, when it became obvious he wasn't going to volunteer the information, I asked with a trace of irritation, "You want to tell me where we're going?"

"Thought you might be a little hungry after that hospital food," he said, a lopsided grin on his face. Words to warm the cockles of my heart, sore throat or not.

"I'm not exactly dressed for the Ritz."

"That's okay," he said, turning from the gravel road into a long, paved driveway, "I don't like snails."

For several minutes we continued to climb a gradual hill. The drive was bracketed by neat lines of barbed-wire fence separating the road from miles of green meadow. Herds of cows looked curiously up to watch us pass by before returning to their grazing. As we cleared the top of the rise, the view took my breath away. Clay pulled to a stop, letting me take in the whole picture.

It looked like one of those scenes from a children's book. At the mouth of a charming little glen stood a perfect red barn, complete with brass weather vane and hayloft. Beyond it, a dock jutted out into a small blue pond. Just visible beyond an apple orchard was a two-story white farmhouse with wraparound porch. The only thing missing was a plume of smoke wisping up from the chimney and a couple of plucky geese. As I watched, a goose waddled across the road.

Clay smiled at my obvious pleasure. "You like it." It wasn't a question.

"If you tell me this is yours, I'm going to demand that you marry me on the spot."

"I only wish," he said, laughing out loud. "This is my grandfather's place. I know you're not in any condition to ride horses, but I hoped you might be up to freshly picked corn on the cob and a thick slice of prime rib."

"Only if you've got horseradish to go with it."

"I might even be able to rustle up some sautéed onions."

"Well, then," I said, waving him on, "what are we waiting for?"

* * *

"When you said fresh picked, I didn't know I was actually going to be the one doing the picking." I had just come back out of the fields, my good arm loaded down with a half-dozen ears of corn.

"Is your arm bothering you?" he asked, hurrying over to take the corn from me. "I shouldn't have you doing field work this soon after getting out of the hospital."

"It's not the field *work* I have a problem with," I said holding out my grungy hands. "It's the field *dirt*."

"Picking your own vegetables is only way to know they're really fresh." Clay laid three thick slabs of excellent beef onto the hot grill. The smell nearly made my eyes water. He flipped the meat, which made a tantalizing sizzle over the hot coals. "Why don't you go in and wash up while I shuck the corn and get it on the grill. Grandpa should be home any time."

"All right. But if you burn that meat, I'll never speak to you again." Heading in the direction Clay had pointed, I entered through the side door of the house into a kitchen to die for. Not that I'd actually know what to do with half of the pots and pans hanging above the butcher block island. But if I were ever going to learn how to cook, that would've been the place to do it.

Leaving the kitchen, I stepped into a well-appointed living room. Expensive furniture was offset by several oil paintings that looked like originals. Clay's grandfather obviously had money.

Being alone, I allowed my natural curiosity to lead me over to a group of trophies on the mantel. Apparently the horses here were show quality. From the mantel, I moved to a cherry-wood bookcase. On the top shelf was a group of framed photos. There was a young Clay standing by a horse nearly twice his size. He was bucktoothed and freckled, but cute as could be. There he was again standing in front of the pond with a string of bulgy-eyed fish. Next to him was an older man who must have been his grandfather.

Something about the older man was familiar. Picking up the frame, I studied the photo from the fading light outside. I'd seen that man before—and recently. I flicked on a nearby light and instantly recognized the face.

Just then, the front door opened, and the man from the picture stepped into the house. He was wearing a dusty cap, but I recognized him immediately. He was the man who had warned me away the first time I'd seen Gam's house.

Clay's grandfather was Pete Blackwood—of Pete's Masonry.

CHAPTER THIRTY-FIVE

"You're Clay's grandfather?"

"Reckon so." Pete closed the front door and stepped into the living room. "And you'd be Elsie's granddaughter. The one I saw up to the house."

I realized I was still holding the picture and set it back on the shelf, feeling like an intruder. "Clay told me I could come in and clean up. I was picking corn," I said, holding out my hands as if to prove my story.

Pete took off his cap and wiped the sweat from his brow. He nodded down the hallway. "Lavatory's that a way."

He watched me all the way into the bathroom. Behind the closed door, I washed my hands, scrubbing at the dirt grimed under my nails, and tried to regain my composure.

Pete was Clay's grandfather. I guess it shouldn't have come as a surprise. Clay had mentioned that his grandfather lived in town. And now that I thought of it, I'd actually seen the barn in the old newspaper photo, and the street we'd turned onto was Hammer Lane. It was just that I couldn't picture the old guy I'd seen driving a beat-up truck, owning a place like this. Masonry must pay better than I thought.

Outside the bathroom, I could hear Clay and his grandfather talking. Displaying my usual nosiness, I pressed my ear to the door but couldn't make out any of their words. At the sound of approaching footsteps, I quickly moved back to the sink.

"Dinner should be ready in about five minutes," Clay called.

"I'll be right out." I studied my face in the mirror. I looked like I'd been through a war. My eyebrows and bangs were singed, matching numerous cuts and scratches across my body. My hair looked like I'd dried it with a leaf blower. And my eyes were still red and irritated from the smoke. All in all, I had no idea why Clay would want to have dinner with me. It must have been a pity date.

Not much I could do about my face, but anything I did to my hair would be an improvement. Taking a brush from my purse, I scooped up a handful of water, and managed to turn myself from a sideshow freak into something a little less hideous than the bride of Frankenstein.

Taking one last look at myself, I grimaced at what I saw and decided that since I probably wouldn't get a second date, I might as well enjoy my meal and not worry about it.

Back outside, Clay had placed the steaks on the top rack of the grill and was turning the corn. "Hope you like your meat rare," he said.

"Just run the cow past an open flame."

"Actually," he said, with a mischievous grin, "these are from a *bull.*"

"How could you know that?" I asked, picturing a grocery store aisle with *his* and *hers* cuts of meat.

"Easy, I helped butcher him. In fact his name was—"

"No!" I shouted, holding up my hands to my ears. "That's going too far. I'm not eating anything with a name.

That would be like watching *Bambi* and then finding out that . . ." I stopped, realizing he was laughing at me.

"You didn't really name it, *did* you?"

"No," he chuckled, his eyes streaming. "We haven't butchered our own meat since I was a kid."

I kicked him in the back of the leg. "If you try to take me snipe hunting after dinner, you're a dead man."

Pretending I'd wounded him, Clay limped over to a nearby chair and waved me to sit beside him. To the west, the sky was turning a bruised purple, and out in the fields frogs and insects were tuning up for their evening chorus. "This is just beautiful," I said.

"Yeah, I come out here whenever I need to unwind."

For the next few minutes, we sat quietly, enjoying the peace of the evening. The night air was beginning to cool, carrying with it a trace of moisture from the nearby lake.

"There's one thing I don't understand," I said. "How can your grandfather afford a place like this by building brick walls or foundations or whatever?"

"Huh?" Clay stared at me confused for a minute before smiling. "Oh you mean the truck? That's just a relic he likes to hang on to. I keep telling him to get rid of it and get something new, but he says he'll keep driving it until he or the truck finally dies."

"So the sign on the side—PETE'S MASONRY?"

"That's as old as the truck. Grandpa's been running the farm full-time since I was a kid." Clay held out both hands, taking in the house and fields around it. "Grandpa bought about six-hundred acres when land here was cheap. He's been selling it off little by little as people come up from the city to build vacation houses."

As if he knew we were talking about him, Pete stumped around from the side of the house carrying a watermelon that must have weighed twenty pounds. "Getting too dang crowded if you ask me," he said, laying the melon onto the patio table.

"Yeah, and you're crying all the way to the bank." Clay turned to me and winked. "Don't get to feeling too sorry for him. He still has more property than he knows what to do with."

"Pretty mouthy for a kid who plans to eat at my table," Pete growled. "Make yourself useful and go get a knife to cut up this melon. I'll take the corn off the grill before you burn it."

Shooting a quick grin over his shoulder, Clay went into the house while his grandfather piled the food onto plates.

"Heard you got yourself into a spot o' trouble up to your grandmother's house this morning," Pete said, his eyes on the plates he was filling. It seemed he had a knack for understatement.

I rubbed my bandaged arm. "That's right."

"Feeling better now, are you?" He began to carry the plates and glasses to the table, and I stood up to help him.

"I'm a little sore," I said lifting several bottles of root beer out of the ice they'd been chilling in. "But I'll survive." I followed him to the table.

"That's good." He took the bottles, still not looking me in the eye.

"When I saw you that day—at Gam's house—you told me you thought I should leave. Just as you were pulling away, you said something else. It sounded like you told me that I might not be safe here."

For several seconds he stood silently, as though he hadn't heard me, then he looked up from the table, his eyes dark and stony. "Might have." He nodded, agreeing with what he'd just said. "Reckon I was right."

"But how could you have known I was in danger?"

His brow furrowed like the lines of a topographical map. "Guess my grandson's kind of sweet on you."

That wasn't the answer I expected, and I could feel my cheeks heat up. I didn't know how to respond.

"That why you're sticking around? 'Cause of him?"

"I'm not sure I understand what you're getting at," I said.

He twisted open a bottle of root beer and poured it into a glass, keeping the head of foam from overflowing the rim. "Told you before," he said, "this place might not be good for you. You decided to stick around anyway, and look what happened. Seems to me you've been through quite a bit, and you're still here. I'm just wondering if that's on account of Clay."

"No." I shook my head. "I just wanted to find out what really happened to Gam." Inside the house, the phone began to ring. Clay must have picked it up, because it cut off halfway through the second ring.

Pete set the bottle on the table, turning it slowly back and forth with the tips of his fingers. "Did you find out the truth about Elsie?"

"I think so."

The weight of his stare was like a physical pressure pushing against me, but I wouldn't look away. Finally he turned and dropped the soda bottles one by one into the trashcan. "Guess you'll be leaving then." His gruff voice sounded almost threatening, but what did he have against me? Why was he in such a hurry to see me go?

"When I'm ready," I said, not telling him Chad had threatened to fire me if I wasn't back at work by Monday.

Almost to spite him, I added, "It's not like I'm in danger *anymore.*"

He looked up abruptly, eyes flashing. I could see his jaw working as it had the first day we first met. Finally, almost too quiet to hear, he said, "Reckon, you thought that the last time too, missy."

I don't know what I would have said—probably something sarcastic—but any response I might have made was cut off by Clay's reappearance. In one hand he was carrying a large butcher knife, in the other a cordless phone. He took the stairs two at a time and walked directly to me.

"That was Sheriff Orr. He checked up on Reggie Torrance. It turns out the guy's got an unshakable alibi for this morning." His face like granite, Clay laid a hand on my shoulder. "Shandra, someone else started that fire."

CHAPTER THIRTY-SIX

"I think you should spend the night here. First thing in the morning, you go back to Salt Lake—at least until we get this all cleared up." Clay sat protectively close to me, his eyes scanning the yard as though some kind of attack were imminent. His attention was both nerve-wracking and reassuring.

"I agree," I said, really meaning it this time. The last few days had drained me of any sense of adventure I might have retained. All I could think about was the safety of my own apartment—the reassurance of my daily routine.

I toyed with my steak, cut off a small slice, and chewed without tasting it. Even my appetite had suffered, a sure sign I was under a lot of pressure. "I just don't understand who would want to hurt me." I looked toward Pete, but he was concentrating on his food, his face unreadable under the patio lights.

"We must have missed something." Clay pushed his plate to one side and laid his steak knife on the table in front of him. "Okay, let's say this is Detective Harding. We can assume that Torrance found out the detective was onto him. That would explain why Torrance killed him."

"But he had no reason to burn down Gam's house if he thought the money was there," I said, leaning across the table.

"Right." Clay took my knife and laid it alongside his own. "This is your grandfather. We won't know conclusively for another day or two if that was *his* body we found in the cellar, but if it was, then the fire might have been an attempt to hide the evidence."

"That's right." I stared at the knives as though they might actually have some kind of clue hidden in the steak juice. "So all we have to do is figure out who killed my grandfather." I stopped abruptly, realizing what I was saying.

Clay looked into my eyes. "What if Torrance was the one who killed your grandfather? When Harding showed up, Torrance hid your grandfather's body and killed the detective. Maybe he went back to the house the night after he threatened you, found the money, and—"

"No." I shook my head, my previous excitement gone. "That can't be it."

"Why not?" He slid the knife forward with his finger. "Whoever killed your grandfather had the motive to start the fire."

Clay's fingers drummed the tabletop with nervous energy, but I laid my hands over them, making sure I had his full attention. "I think I know who killed my grandfather."

"You do?"

"It was . . ." I swallowed hard. Even though I'd reached the conclusion myself, saying it to someone else was much harder than I thought it would be. "I think it was my grandmother."

Pete looked up sharply. Clay stared at me as though he thought I was pulling some kind of practical joke. All around us the sounds of the night continued uninterrupted, but at the table there was only silence.

"Are you sure?" Clay asked.

I coughed nervously into my hand. "Pretty sure, yeah." It was time I told someone what I knew.

"I imagine she felt like it was self-defense . . . and maybe it was. I guess we'll never really know." Steeling myself against the feeling that I was being disloyal to Gam's memory, I told Clay everything I knew—starting with what happened to my mother and even relating Mrs. Steven's story that Gam might have taken a lover.

"So when my grandfather showed up with the money from the robbery, he must have thought she'd take him back. He didn't know she'd stopped loving him the day he attacked my mother, if not before. Maybe he threatened her. Maybe she just decided she'd had enough. Either way, the result was the same. She killed him in her bedroom. She must've panicked, because she didn't even try to hide the body. Just left the house she loved and never came back."

Clay leaned back in his chair and ran his fingers through his hair. "And it's been up there all this time? Over twenty years?"

I nodded silently.

"And you didn't know any of this before you came here?"

"No," I whispered. "I didn't know, and I didn't want to believe it when I heard it. Gam's been there for me all my life. She was even closer to me than my mother. Up until this week, I'd have sworn there wasn't a violent bone in her body. But I have to face the facts. Whether I like it or not, my grandmother killed my grandfather."

Clay wrapped his fingers around mine, an offer of comfort. He opened his mouth to speak, but before he could say a word, Pete stood, knocking his chair over backward. In the moonlight, his eyes glowed wide and white.

Watching him stand before me, his arms shaking and mouth working, I first thought that he was suffering some kind of attack. Clay reached toward his grandfather, but Pete knocked his hand away.

"You don't know anything!" The old man shouted at me, spittle flying from the corners of his mouth. "You think you're so smart, but you don't know a cotton pickin' thing."

Stunned by the sudden explosiveness of his outburst, I sat pressed against the back of my chair.

"Granddad?" Clay stammered.

Ignoring his grandson, Pete stomped around the table toward me. As he closed the distance between us, I could see that his face had gone alarmingly pale. Hectic, brick-red circles stood out on each cheek. He raised one hand in the air, and for a moment I was sure he was going to strike me with it. Instead, he pointed a knobby index finger into my face, swinging it up and down like a sword.

"Let me tell you something," he said, his voice high-pitched and trembling. "I knew you brought trouble with you first time I laid eyes on you. Told you to make tracks, but you wouldn't listen. Folks was fine till you showed up. Kept their ideas to themselves until you poked a stick in their nest and got 'em all riled up."

He was running out of wind, and his Adam's apple bobbed up and down as he tried to catch his breath, but he was determined to have his say. Bending over slightly, hands pressed to his hips, he glared at me. "You got no right," he puffed into my face. "No right to say them kinds of things. You don't know what you're talking about, and you do the dead a grave wrong."

He dropped one hand to the table and slumped backward. If Clay hadn't been there to catch him, he might have fallen to the ground. Instead, Clay half carried, half dragged him back to his chair.

Pete's shouting had frightened the wildlife around us into silence. As the three of us looked at each other—Pete and I sitting, Clay standing at his grandfather's side—the night was as quiet as a graveyard. I tried to understand what I might have done to upset the old man so much. Slowly, understanding dawned on me.

I pulled my chair close to his and looked into his wrinkled face. "Are you saying that Gam . . ."

He raised his hands to his face, scrubbing the jutting shelves of his cheekbones. His voice was soft, but in the silence of the night, it carried well enough. "Elsie never did nothing like that. She never killed a soul."

CHAPTER THIRTY-SEVEN

Without another word, Pete placed a hand on the table, pulled himself up, and walked away. I glanced questioningly at Clay. He shrugged his shoulders, and we both followed his grandfather across the patio and into the darkness. For a man as old as he was, Pete moved with surprising speed and confidence.

Bereft of any light but the moon, I could barely see a thing. I stuck close to Clay, waiting for my eyes to adjust. When they did, I could see we were following a small dirt path. The path dropped down the side of a gentle hill, where I could see the reflection of the pond below.

At the edge of the water, Pete stooped and picked up something from the ground. He reached back and side armed a rock out across the pond. It skipped several times before disappearing beneath the surface with a hollow *bloop*. He threw again, and another rock skimmed out over the water.

Clay placed a hand on the old man's shoulder. "Granddad?"

Pete bounced his fist gently against his pant leg. The rocks still in his hand rattled against one another like dice. Without turning, he said, "You want to know who killed Stewart?"

"I do," Clay said.

"And if I tell you, you're going to want to arrest him?" He drew the words out slowly, as though it hurt to speak them.

Clay squeezed his grandfather's arm. "Can you give me any reason why I shouldn't?"

Pete tossed another rock, but this one sunk immediately into the black water. His head dropped and his shoulders slumped. "Sometimes a fellow does a thing that he wished later he hadn't done. It might be a just thing, maybe even the right thing. But in the eyes of the law it's still wrong."

Was he saying what I thought he was saying? Clay turned toward me, his eyes silver in the moonlight, and I knew he was wondering the same thing. It sounded as though Pete was about to confess to the murder of my grandfather.

"This person," Clay said. "Could he have burned down Elsie's house to cover his tracks?"

"Reckon so," Pete said.

Clay turned his grandfather toward him. "Granddad, maybe you'd better get a lawyer before you say anything more."

"A lawyer?" Pete looked sharply up. "What in tarnation for?"

"I'm sworn to uphold the law," Clay said carefully as though speaking to a six year old. "Anything you tell me could be used against you in court."

"Against *me*?" Pete waved away a cloud of gnats congregating around his head. "What would I be doing in court?"

Clay glanced toward me with a look of exasperation, and then back at his grandfather. "If you killed someone, I have to arrest you, Granddad. Even if you thought it was the right thing to do. There's no way to get around that."

"What are you talking about, boy? I never killed no one." Pete chuffed. He scowled in my direction. "And don't let nobody tell you different."

"Then who?" Clay and I asked almost simultaneously.

Pete muttered something that sounded like "hornet's nest" and threw the rest of the rocks he was holding into the water, where they created a dozen overlapping ripples. He folded his hands over his chest, staring out across the pond.

"Elsie Sullivan was the prettiest girl Echo Lake ever saw," Pete said, a wistful melancholy in his voice. "Us fellows used to chase her around after school and carve her initials in trees when no one was looking. Always kind of figured she had a hankering for me. I'd dance with her at the Saturday night cotillions. She was light as a feather and so full of energy, she left all of us suitors gasping."

I tried to imagine my grandmother as a young woman dancing the night away, but I couldn't quite pull it off. Suddenly I wondered if the dress I'd seen had actually been Gam's and not my mother's at all.

"Reckon she'd always had her sights set on an *away* fellow, though." The trace smile that had crept over Pete's wrinkled face as he recalled dancing with my grandmother disappeared.

"Stewart Brecken came to town throwing around dollar bills like they were candy wrappers. Folks around here thought he was loaded, but it turned out he was a working stiff like everyone else. He'd just finished a job building some big housing project down a city, and the money was burning holes in his pockets.

"Most of us boys was off fighting the North Koreans at the time, so Stewart had his pick of the crop. He was older than the rest of us, and he'd done his time in World War II. I heard about Elsie's engagement in a letter from my mother. By the time I got home, she was already married and with a bun in the oven."

"What does this have to do with—" Clay began to ask.

Pete cut him off with a look that could boil water. "You want to hear this or not?"

Clay held up his hands in surrender, and Pete continued.

"Didn't have anything against Brecken personally. He just did what the rest of us only wished we could do when he took Elsie as his wife. I'll admit it burned me up when I first heard she'd married someone else, but we all got home from the war and got on with our lives. I married my Janey—may she rest in peace—and started up the masonry business.

"Folks around here never did take on too well with Elsie's out-of-town husband though. They still liked Elsie, but they never really trusted Stewart. Might've been the way he talked like he was big stuff, or how quick he was to use his fists on someone he disagreed with. Mostly, I guess, we just didn't trust him. He never really looked you in the eye when he talked to you or gave a good, firm handshake the way most fellows do.

"Wasn't nobody really surprised when they heard how Elsie'd finally run him off. We could see the bruises easy enough for ourselves, and everybody knew he'd been hitting the bottle pretty hard. He wasn't the only man who showed up to church with the smell of whiskey on his breath, but we all felt protective of Elsie, and we'd have stood up to him in a heartbeat if she'd asked us to."

Pete turned to me, rubbing the back of his neck. "Guess what Nan told you about Stewart and your mother was true. Didn't see it myself of course, but word kind of got around, and Elsie never denied it. Everybody was real sorry to hear what happened to your grandmother, and we all tried to help out—dropping off vegetables at her house, fixing things that needed fixing, and such. If we'd have gotten our hands on Stewart after that, he'd never have made it out of town alive I reckon."

"But he did come back," I said, feeling goose pimples raise on my arms and neck.

"Guess so," he said. "Again, never saw him myself, but I hear things."

"And someone killed him?" Clay asked, his voice low.

"Yup." Pete nodded.

"So you're saying his body's been lying in that house for twenty years and no one knew it?" Clay stared at his grand-father as if Pete had just admitted to being the tooth fairy.

"'Course not." Pete said, giving Clay a withering glare. "Lots of folks knew what happened. That's why we kept people away from her house."

"But if Elsie didn't kill him . . ." Clay looked confused again, but I thought I knew the answer.

"It was her lover, wasn't it?"

Pete shifted his feet, the joints in his knees cracking. Again he looked out over the pond—perhaps at one of the distant twinkling stars. "Not in the sense folks use that word today," he said. "Elsie'd lost her husband, but she never cheated on him. Folks just kind of pitched in to help her out. One person would bring her a pail of milk. Another would bring some chicken they'd fried too much of. Just helping out until she could get back on her feet.

"Turned out Elsie was plenty able to take care of herself and her daughter. They grew their own garden. Raised chickens. Elsie made some of the finest afghans you ever saw. They got by just fine. Pretty soon folks let them be.

"Only one fellow kept coming around to help out. Everyone knew he was sweet on Elsie, and I guess she liked him okay too. But they never let it go past friendship. People who didn't know any better might have talked, but if they so much as held hands, I never saw it, and I drove by that house four or five times every day."

"Why didn't she just divorce Stewart?" I asked. The night was starting to take on a real chill, and we'd need to go inside soon.

"Divorce was a dirty word back then, especially in little Utah towns like this. I don't guess proper women got divorced, even if their husbands were lower than dirt."

Clay cleared his throat, obviously wanting to get back to the murder. "You're saying that when Stewart came back, this other man killed him?"

Pete nodded.

"But if Elsie didn't kill her husband, why did she run?"

Pete only scowled, but again I thought I knew the answer, and it nearly broke my heart. "She left because she didn't want to see the killer go to jail. She gave up everything she loved so he wouldn't get arrested."

"Reckon that's about right," Pete said, his voice gruff with emotion.

"And she never came back. She couldn't come back for fear of putting him in danger, so she never saw the man she really loved again." It was like one of those tragic romances where the lovers are so close to one another but might as well be worlds apart for all the good it did them.

"And he's still here?" Clay said.

"Yeah, he's here."

"Who?" Clay asked. "Who is he?"

Pete heaved a sigh that seemed to originate from miles beneath his feet. He wiped his hand across his brow and, in words so quiet they were nearly inaudible above the sounds of the frogs and insects around us, said, "Trevor Baptista."

CHAPTER THIRTY-EIGHT

"Who?" I don't know what I was expecting, but it certainly wasn't this. The name Baptista meant nothing to me, though I had a vague sense that I might have heard of a Trevor somewhere.

"That drunk?" At Clay's words, I remembered why Trevor sounded familiar.

"The old man in the jail."

"Right," said Clay, "but why would he—"

"He's the one in the woods, isn't he?" I said, turning to Pete.

Clay looked confused, but Pete nodded.

Now I understood. "That's what he was doing by Gam's house—making sure that no one went in. When I came back from the lake, I stumbled on his camp."

"Is this something else you didn't tell me about?" Clay asked. He was obviously exasperated, but I was too excited to worry about it.

"Don't you see?" I said to Clay. "He couldn't leave the house for fear someone would find the body. And Gam couldn't come back for fear of the same thing."

"Why would your grandmother care what happened to an old drunk?"

Next to the pond, Pete harrumphed. "Wasn't always a drunk. Used to be a good man, one of the finest carpenters around. Better than Stewart even."

"I'll bet that's how he met Gam. He worked with my grandfather didn't he? I'll bet he was one of the men I saw in the newspaper picture."

"He was Stewart's partner." Pete's voice sounded tired, defeated. "With Elsie and your mother on their own, he used to stop by their house all the time—fixing what needed to be fixed, buying toys for little Trinity. Stewart drank like a fish toward the end, but I never saw Trevor take anything stronger than soda pop until . . ."

"Until he killed my grandfather." I finished for him.

"Until then." Pete folded his arms across his chest "He went downhill fast after that."

Pete picked up a handful of pebbles and tossed them out into the water. "So what are you going to do?" he asked Clay.

"What else *can* I do?" Clay said. "He's responsible for at least one murder, not to mention arson, and the attempted murder of Shandra. I'm going to call the sheriff, and we're going to arrest him."

Pete shot me a dark look, but it didn't seem to carry much strength. He shook his head and muttered. "Never should have come here."

* * *

The chains of the front porch swing creaked softly as I rocked back and forth. In the moonlight, the barn and everything around it was transformed into shades of silver and black. Clay came around the side of the house, hands in his pockets, and stood looking down at me.

"Aren't you cold?"

"No," I said, holding out the sleeves of an old, gray cardigan that hung a good four inches past the tips of my fingers. "Your grandfather loaned me one of his sweaters."

Clay nodded. "I talked to the sheriff. We're going to wait until morning to arrest Trevor."

"That's probably the best way."

He looked out on the moonlit countryside, rocking from the heels of his boots to the toes and back again along with the swing.

"Would you like to sit?" I asked.

"I have to get into the office. I'm on graveyard tonight."

"Oh."

"But I guess I've got a few minutes."

I scooted to one side, and he sat beside me. Our legs brushed against each other as the swing moved forward and back, and I was acutely aware of each touch. I tried to think of something to say, but every idea seemed more lame than the one before it, so I settled for saying nothing.

Clay finally broke the silence. "I guess you're pretty glad to find out that your grandmother didn't kill your grandfather after all."

"I am," I said, brushing the toes of my sneakers along the boards of the porch. "But at the same time, I feel sorry for Trevor. He seemed like a nice guy."

"I guess sometimes love makes people do crazy things."

"I guess." I couldn't imagine loving someone enough to kill for them, but maybe that perspective would change if I met the right guy. "I just wish you didn't have to arrest the poor man."

"He nearly killed you. If I hadn't found you when I did, you would have died in that fire."

In the darkness I turned. I don't know if Clay leaned toward me, or I toward him—or maybe it was a little of both—but suddenly I found myself kissing him. In the cold night air, his lips were fire against mine. He put a hand on my shoulder, and inside my sneakers, my toes curled.

For the few seconds our lips pressed together, everything else seemed to stop. The motion of the swing, the sounds of the night—even my heart seemed to stop its beating until he pulled back.

"Wow," I whispered, trying to catch my breath.

"Yeah." He seemed as surprised by the kiss as I was. Had it been a mistake? We lived hours away from each other, and we'd only known one another for a few days.

"I need to get inside," I said, sounding like I'd just run a mile.

"And I need to get into work." He stood up. "Sheriff hates it when I'm late."

I didn't want it to be a mistake. "Clay . . ."

He grabbed my shoulders and pulled me toward him. Again we kissed, and every pain, every worry, every fear left me.

"Be careful," I said, heat running through my veins like molten lava.

"I will." As he pulled out his keys and walked toward his car, I wondered whether his feet felt as far above the ground as mine did.

CHAPTER THIRTY-NINE

I woke to golden bars of late morning sunlight glowing through the plantation shutters of my bedroom window. If this farm had a rooster, he'd fallen down on the job—or, more than likely, I'd just slept through his wakeup call. Still, I hadn't felt this relaxed in a long time. After a luxuriously long shower, I padded into the kitchen and found a note on the table.

Shandra,

We've gone to arrest Trevor. Your car is parked out front, but DO NOT go anywhere near the remains of your grandmother's house until we have this guy behind bars. Also, please don't leave without seeing me first. I've been thinking about you all night.

Clay

P.S. Granddad's out working on fences, so just help yourself to breakfast. Eggs and bacon are in the fridge.

I ran my finger across the words *I've been thinking about you all night*. I'd been thinking about him too. It had been a long time since I'd felt like this, and honestly, I was a little unsure of myself. Was this one of those things where we'd phone each other for a while after I went home and then eventually forget to call—like the summer vacation romances you have when you're a kid that fade away into fond memories? Was I just reacting to his having saved my life? Did I even want it to be more serious than that? Did *he* want it to be more?

I opened the fridge and took out four eggs, cheddar cheese, some green onions, and six slices of bacon. I might have mentioned that I think better on a full stomach. As I sprinkled cheddar cheese over the eggs—my tummy rumbling like a freight train at the aroma—I found myself whistling "Happy Days Are Here Again." Okay, so maybe I *did* want to follow this romance thing at least a little further.

After wolfing down my breakfast, I took my things out to the car and put them in the trunk. Royce's trunk isn't very big, but fortunately I didn't have much stuff. Having no idea when Clay would be back, I figured I might as well take a tour of the farm.

In the far distance, I could see Pete's truck parked out at the edge of a large field. I thought I could just make him out, kneeling by the barbed-wire fence. Closer to me was the barn, at least as tall as a three-story building and painted a bright red with white trim. I walked through the big double doors. Inside, the air was suffused with the smells of hay, tractor oil, leather, and a hundred other things that all said farm.

Running my hand along a row of well-oiled saddles and bridles, my thoughts returned to Trevor. There were a million questions I wanted to ask him. If only I'd known who he was when we were jail mates—there where so many things he might have told me. What really happened between him and Gam? Had he killed my grandfather in self-defense? If he got sent to prison, I might never get the chance to ask him.

At the other side of the barn, the smells abruptly changed to something just as farm-like but much less appealing. Through the second set of double doors, I could see a rusty semi trailer, which was undoubtedly loaded with manure. Quickly detouring away from the trailer, I headed toward a tree-lined stream with several horses grazing nearby.

Another thing still bothering me was Reggie Torrance, my grandfather's partner in the bank robbery. He didn't strike me as the most intelligent guy in the world, and I could certainly see him killing the detective to protect his identity. But what was the deal with the footprints? He hadn't admitted anything, and no one had come up with a satisfactory theory on why there were no footprints other than the detective's and my own.

Halfway to the stream I stopped. Clay had warned me away from Gam's house plot, but he hadn't said anything about the sheriff's office. If I went by now, maybe I could talk to Trevor and Torrance before they were transported to the county jail. Would the sheriff let me talk to him? The worst he could say was no.

* * *

When I reached the sheriff's office, the door was locked. A cold wind was blowing pregnant clouds across the sky. I imagined that Clay and Sheriff Orr were out looking for Trevor. Across the street, Big Mike's was doing a brisk lunch hour business. The smell of frying meat emanating from the diner was irresistible. I'd get a quick lunch and then check back in at the station before going home.

Inside the diner, I saw that Nan was working. She gestured toward an empty table. "How you doing, hon?"

I tilted my hand back and forth in the air. "I've done better."

She glanced over her shoulder at the young waitress on duty. "Chilly, can you take my tables for a couple minutes?" The waitress nodded.

Nan slid onto the bench across from me. "I heard about the house."

"I lost everything."

"Not your memories."

I looked outside at the fast-moving clouds. It was going to storm good and hard before the day was over. I wanted to be on the road before then. "The memories I'm taking home with me aren't exactly the memories I'd hoped for," I said.

"Are they ever?" Nan picked up my menu, tapping it against her hand for emphasis as she spoke. "We build up these impossible fantasies in our minds—ideas of who we really are—who our parents are. Tell me one little girl who hasn't secretly dreamed she's a princess who was adopted by a middle-class family. But the truth is we have to live with the hand we were dealt. For every negative thing you've heard, there are a hundred positive ones you've missed."

"Like what?" I felt as though I'd been hammered over the head with nothing but bad news since I'd arrived.

"Oh, a million things." Nan pulled a rag out of her apron and began to scrub at the tabletop. "Like how your grandmother was the most generous woman in the world. Even when she didn't have a cent to her name, she'd find a way to do for others. And how your mother wrote the most beautiful poetry. I imagine you got your writing talent from her. Your father couldn't write a lick, but I swear he made me laugh every time I saw him. He just had a natural way of finding the ridiculous in everyday things. He could have been one of those standup comics if he'd wanted. Why, even your grandfather had his good points."

"But I have nothing to remember them by. All Gam's things are gone, and my mother died when I was only nine. And I barely remember my father at all."

Nan stood, placing her work-reddened hands flat on the table. She leaned down and looked into my eyes. "I'm going to get you the biggest, juiciest burger you ever ate. You look like you've lost at least five pounds since you were in here last—and you didn't have much meat on you to begin with.

"First, though, I want to tell you something I hope you'll remember. I don't claim to know everything that happened between your mom and dad. Maybe you'll figure it all out one day, and maybe you won't. But I do know that they were good people. I can see a lot of their best traits in you. So anytime you want to see your parents, you just look in the mirror. They'd both be awfully proud of how you've turned out. And that's more important than anything you might have lost in the fire.

With that, she turned and hurried back into the kitchen. She was right—it was the juiciest burger I'd ever eaten.

CHAPTER FORTY

Trevor looked much as I'd remembered him. A sweater even grungier and more patched than the rest of his clothing covered his dirty shirt. He was sitting on the edge of his cot, shoulders slumped, downturned head resting in his wrinkled hands. He didn't bother to look up as Clay and I approached his cell.

Clay glanced at me, silently asking if I still wanted to go through with this. When I nodded, he rapped his knuckles on the outside of the bars. "Someone here to see you, Trevor."

The old man raised his head. His eyes were still bloodshot, but the animation I'd seen in them before was gone. They looked empty, lifeless. For a second I thought I saw a spark of recognition before he dropped his head back into his palms.

I knelt beside the bars, bringing my face to the level of his. "Do you remember me, Trevor?"

There was no response.

"I'm Shandra Covington. Elsie's granddaughter."

He grunted without looking up.

"Trevor," I said gently, as though trying to coax a timid mouse out of its hole. "Did you know my grandmother?"

He raised his head a fraction, just enough to peek out at me from behind his shaggy brows. "Sure, I did."

"You were her friend."

One dirt-crusted hand dropped to his knee, rubbing at fabric so thin it was almost transparent. "We was friends."

Wrapping my fingers around the cold cell bars, afraid that he would shut down again, I tried to hold his eyes with mine. "You helped my grandmother, didn't you?" Beside me, Clay shifted restlessly.

Trevor raised his head a little higher. His tongue darted out to wet his lips. "I heped her."

"How did you help her, Trevor?"

"Fixed stuff. Mowed the grass." A weak smile creased his leathery face. "I took care of things."

"You did," I said, returning his smile. "You took care of her." There was something in this man—an essential goodness buried beneath the years of alcohol and neglect.

"Is that what happened?" I asked. "Were you protecting Gam from my grandfather?"

Trevor glanced warily toward Clay.

"You might as well tell her," Clay said, a little more harshly than I would have liked. "You've already admitted to everyone else that you killed Stewart Brecken."

Trevor's head dropped. His eyes disappeared from view. "Thas right." I could barely hear his voice. "I kilt Stewart." Something about the way he pronounced *killed* as *kilt,* prompted a memory, but for the life of me I couldn't remember why.

Clay spoke again. "You killed him and left his body in the house. That's why Elsie had to leave."

I tried to catch Clay's eyes, silently begging him to leave Trevor alone. I could feel the old man drawing back into his shell, shutting down. Clay, concentrating on Trevor, missed my look.

"Thas right," Trevor said, his voice lifeless. "I left 'im there."

Something had been troubling me ever since Pete admitted that Trevor had killed my grandfather. "Why did you wait all those years to move the body? Why leave it in Gam's house when you could have moved it anytime you wanted to?"

Trevor looked up, his eyes tired and confused. He glanced from me to Clay and then back again. "I left it there."

"But why move it after all this time? Was it because you saw me go into Gam's house?"

Trevor sucked in his lower lip, displaying his toothless and blackened gums. "Thas right," he said, finally. "Seen you go in." Again his eyes darted to Clay. Was there something he was afraid to say in front of the police?

"Clay, could you give us a minute or two alone?"

Clay shook his head. "I really shouldn't—"

"Just for a minute. You could stand down the hall, and we'd still be in sight."

Clay looked toward Sheriff Orr's office at the end of the hall. "I guess I could do that—just for a minute or two. Stay away from the bars, and if he tries anything—anything at all—call me."

"I will. I promise." I waited for Clay to walk to the end of the hall before turning to Trevor.

"Is there anything you want to tell me?" I asked.

Trevor wiped his nose with the sleeve of his sweater. "Nope. Got nothing ta say."

He was hiding something. But what? I tried another tack. "When you moved my grandfather's body, where did you hide it?"

"Put it inna basement," he responded immediately.

"Why? Why not hide it in the woods?"

He shrugged, his bony shoulders coming almost to his ears.

His clam routine was really beginning to get under my skin. "Listen," I said, pressing my face against the bars of Trevor's cell, "that fire you set in Gam's house destroyed everything. It burned up links between my family and me that I can never get back. For a few minutes I actually felt like I had a past—and you took it away. And you nearly killed me. Don't you think I deserve an explanation? Don't I at least deserve that?"

Heat burned against the backs of my eyes, but I forced myself to blink it away. I squeezed the bars until my hands looked like white gloves.

"Tell me." I begged. "Tell me the truth."

Trevor shook his head, tears gleaming in his eyes. "No. No, no, no. I never done that. I'd never torch her house. I loved her."

"Then who? If you didn't start the fire, who did?" If I could have pulled the bars apart with my bare hands and climbed into the cell with him, I would have. I was so close to whatever it was the old man was hiding.

"Is everything okay?" Hearing the commotion, Clay had returned to my side. He placed his hands on my shoulders. In his cell, Trevor tucked his face back into his palms, rocking back and forth on his bunk like a child.

"Please," I said. "Why won't you tell me, Trevor?"

"All done talking," he muttered through his closed fingers. "All done, all done, all done, all done."

I stood up, sick to death of the whole mess. "Let's go."

* * *

"You can't blame the old guy. His brain's so pickled, it's a wonder he even remembers his name." Clay fed a handful of coins into the soda machine and bought an orange pop for each of us.

"You're probably right," I said, pulling the tab on my can. "It's just . . ." I paused with the soda halfway to my mouth.

"What is it?"

I set the drink back on the table. "When we were talking to Trevor, he said he'd killed Stewart. Only he pronounced it *kilt*, like what they wear in Scotland."

"And?" Clay drained half his can in a single slug.

"I thought it sounded familiar, but I couldn't remember why. Now I do. When I was in jail with him, he said that he'd never *kilt* anyone before."

"So he lied."

"Maybe, but . . ." I tried to recall the exact conversation we'd had. I'd just told him I was in jail for killing someone, and he said that he'd never killed anyone himself. He'd said . . . I dredged my memory for his exact words. "He said that he hadn't killed anyone, but he wished that he had. Something about not having the guts to do it."

"Shandra." Clay reached across the table and took my hand. "You don't want to see Trevor go to prison, and neither do I. He's an old drunk who probably won't last twelve more months. But the fact is, he's confessed to killing your grandfather, and he nearly killed you. He needs to be locked up."

"I know." I studied Clay's eyes, wishing I had his confidence that this was the right thing. "I just keep feeling like we're missing something."

Releasing my hand, Clay stood. "Before you leave, I've got something for you." He smiled, an anticipatory gleam in his eyes. "Wait here."

"Okay." I sat at the graffiti-scarred table, playing with my soda can and trying not to think about how Trevor would undoubtedly die behind bars.

After a minute or two, Clay came back into the room holding something tucked behind his back. He smiled almost shyly down at me. "I know how much those things of your grandmother's meant to you."

"Don't remind me," I said, thinking that the scars of losing Gam's things would last a lot longer than the cuts and bruises I'd received in the fire.

"Maybe this will help a little." From behind his back, Clay withdrew Gam's music box—the duplicate of the one I had at home—and placed it in my hands.

I opened the lid of the box, and the tiny dancers twirled along to the music. "Don't you need to keep this for evidence or something?"

"Nope. It turns out the music box wasn't the murder weapon after all."

"It wasn't?"

"Torrance damaged the box to make it look like he'd used it to kill Detective Harding," Clay said, pointing to a corner where the wood had pulled apart. "But the real weapon was a pipe we found in his motel room."

I shut the box, and the music stopped with a click. I knew just where I'd keep it. On the dresser in my apartment, right beside the one that had belonged to my mother. "Thank you." I stood up and hugged Clay's neck as hard as I could. "You have no idea how much this means to me."

CHAPTER FORTY-ONE

As we stepped out of the station house, a roar of thunder pealed across the sky. The afternoon had gone dark gray beneath a cover of menacing black clouds, and the air was filled with the kind of static electricity you can taste in the back of your mouth. As if to prove the clouds meant business, a fat raindrop splattered against the sidewalk in front of me.

"Let me walk you to your car." Clay took off his jacket and held it above my head.

"No. There's no point in both of us getting wet."

He put his jacket back on and pulled me into another hug. I wondered if he'd kiss me again, but he didn't. It was all right. The magic of the night before was still fresh in my mind, and I figured we both needed time to sort through our feelings.

"Just make sure you come back and visit, huh?" He whispered in my ear. I nodded, a small, secret smile on my face. Tucking the music box under my sweatshirt, I dashed to the car.

Safe inside, I set the music box on the seat beside me. The wood on the corner had pulled apart in several places, and a dark stain marred the finish, but I would still cherish it forever. I glanced toward the station house, but he was already gone. I wondered if I'd ever be back. It felt like Clay and I might have something together, but only time would tell.

Above me a bolt of lightning knifed across the black clouds, and three more large drops exploded against the windshield. If I didn't hit the road soon, I was going to get soaked. I put the key in the ignition, turned it, and— nothing happened. I tried again. Nothing. Not even a measly little click.

"Please, not now," I begged, studying the dark sky. I pumped the gas pedal a couple of times and jiggled the key—the limit of my mechanical knowledge. "Come on, baby." Crossing my fingers, I tried the ignition again. No luck.

"Okay, you know what, Royce? I really don't need this." I got out of the car and opened the hood. A gust of wind shook the car, nearly pulling the hood from my hands before I could get it locked in place. As far as I could tell, everything looked fine. But then again, I couldn't tell the carburetor from the Terminator.

Every couple of months, Bobby urges me to take an auto repair class. "If you're going to drive that bucket of bolts, you should really learn how to work on it." Royce and I had managed to hold him off so far, but now I wished I'd taken his advice. I considered wiggling a few wires for the heck of it and decided I'd probably do more damage than good.

"Got a problem?" Without even looking up, I recognized the rough voice that called out to me, and the clack-clack-clack of the even rougher engine.

"My car won't start," I shouted to Pete over the racket of his engine.

"Lemme take a look." As Pete climbed out of his truck, the clouds overhead boomed again, warning anyone stupid enough to still be standing outside that a serious storm was about to commence.

"Got gas in her?" He asked, pulling his cap down tight against his forehead.

"I filled it this morning." The wind whipped my words away as soon as they left my mouth.

Pete studied the workings of my little car's engine like he knew what he was doing. "Got an awful lot of corrosion on your battery cables." I nodded as though I'd been thinking just the same thing. He twisted what I assumed to be the battery cables back and forth a few times, breaking loose a coating of something green and powdery.

"Try it now," he shouted.

I ran around to the driver's seat and turned the key. Pete watched me from his position next to the front fender of the car. Nothing happened. I raised my hands, palms up.

He nodded and disappeared beneath the hood again. After a minute he popped back out. "Try her again."

I considered telling him that Royce was a *he*, but decided this might not be the time. I tried the key with no more success than the first two tries. "Still nothing," I said as he came around to the door.

"Battery's probably dead." He shrugged, eyeing the sky. "Why don't you lock her up, and I'll drive you to a guy who can fix it."

I grabbed my keys and reached for the music box—not wanting to take a chance on losing it again. As I hurried around the front of Pete's truck and pulled open the heavy door, the raindrops turned from onesies and twosies to a full downpour.

"Looks like this is going to be quite a storm," I said, wiping the water from my face.

"We can use the water." He wrestled the truck into first gear and pulled back into the street. Through the water streaming down the windows, the lights from Main Street's buildings looked like portholes in a passing ship. Pete switched on his windshield wipers. The ancient blades did little more than move the water around, making it almost impossible to see clearly more than a few yards ahead. At least we had the road pretty much to ourselves, and Pete appeared comfortable keeping the needle of his speedometer between fifteen and twenty, so I didn't figure we were in much danger.

"You think this guy will be able to fix my car today?" I asked. "I really need to be back at work."

"Reckon so," Pete said, never taking his eyes from the road. "I could drop you off at the mechanic here in town. But he charges an arm and a leg and doesn't know a torque wrench from a monkey wrench. Fellow I know does a good job at a fair price, but he's down the road apiece."

"Just as long as he can get me on the road again today."

"If anyone can, he can."

With nothing else to do, I studied the broken corner of my music box, wondering if it would be possible to get it fixed. The wood had been shattered where the sides dovetailed with the bottom. Something white—maybe unstained wood—showed through the crack.

"You talk to Trevor?" Pete asked, ignoring a minivan that tailgated us for a minute before zipping around to the left and passing.

"Yeah." I tried fitting the broken pieces of wood back together in what appeared to be a lost cause.

"What'd he say?"

"He admitted that he killed my grandfather, but that was about it."

Pete grunted noncommittally, easing the truck to the right as another car passed.

"You know, the thing that still bothers me is the footprints," I said, turning the music box in my hands like a Rubik's Cube. "Either Torrance moved my grandfather's body for some unknown reason when he killed the detective, or Trevor moved it to hide his crime. But how did he manage to do it without leaving any footprints? And what would have been the point?"

"Don't know," Pete said, his eyes still glued to the road.

"And here's another thing. Torrance figured the money was in the house, so if he was already in the house with the detective, why not search for the money while he was there?" As I pressed against the side of the box, I felt the wood give a little beneath my fingers. Maybe I could push it back together after all.

"Afraid of gettin' caught?" Pete suggested.

I pressed a little harder against the wood, and suddenly the whole base of the music box seemed to collapse beneath the pressure of my fingers. "Darn!"

"What's wrong?" Pete spared a quick glance in my direction.

"I think I just broke Gam's music—" I stopped, stunned by what I was seeing. I hadn't broken the music box at all; I'd released some kind of hidden compartment built into its base. I pulled the compartment open.

Tucked inside was a slim stack of time-faded envelopes. Pulling the letters from the compartment, I fanned quickly through them. Each was addressed to Elsie Brecken. The return addresses varied from one letter to the next, but the sender was the same. All of them were from . . . Stewart Brecken.

CHAPTER FORTY-TWO

"Whatcha got there?" Pete slowed the truck a little, craning his neck to see what I was holding.

"Letters," I said, showing him the stack. "They're all from my grandfather."

"'Fore he left?"

I checked the date stamps on the envelopes. "No. *After* he left." The earliest was dated December 22, 1964—the year Gam ran him out of town. The most recent was February 21, 1984—a week after my grandfather and Torrance robbed the First Central Credit Union. He'd been writing to her all the time he was gone, and she'd kept each letter.

I opened the first envelope. The paper inside was stiff with age, and the straggling handwriting was a little faded, but I had no trouble reading it.

Dearest Elsie,

I know I've done you wrong. I regret that I ever laid a hand on you and little Trinity, and you were right to throw me out. But I swear I never touched our daughter like you think I did. Please see it in your heart to let me come home.

Love always,

Stewart

I flipped the page over, but that was it. Pete was glancing quizzically in my direction. I held the letter out for him to see.

He shook his head. "Can't see nothing smaller'n a horsefly without my specs. What's it say?"

I read it to him.

"Harrumph," he said. Up until that point I'd never actually heard someone say *harrumph*. I thought it was just one of those words you read in books, but there it was.

"You don't believe him?" I asked.

"Man'll say anything to get his house and family back."

I couldn't say that I disagreed. Sliding the letter back into its envelope, I moved on to the next, written about a year later. It was more of the same. No information about where he was or what he was doing—just a plea to let him come home and a denial that he'd abused my mother. The third and fourth were almost exact duplicates, written two and three years apart.

"Why would she keep these?" I said, mostly to myself.

"Probably for toilet paper," Pete offered, chuckling to himself.

I continued to read the letters as Pete drove through the premature night. Each was more or less the same as the one before it, although the time span between had lengthened. Nothing changed until the second to the last.

"Listen to this," I said, holding the paper near the dashboard light to see better. "'After all of these years without you

I've got some good news at last. I spoke with a friend today who knows a man that witnessed everything on that night many years ago. He will testify that I did not molest Trinity. Even better, he will tell me who did. The man wants money to tell his story, but I think I know how I can get it. I will speak with him soon and should be able to prove my innocence at last.'"

I handled the letter gingerly. *Prove my innocence.* Was there a chance my grandfather *had* been telling the truth?

"Pete, do you know who my grandfather might have been talking about?"

"No idea," Pete said, looking as surprised as I felt. He switched on the defroster to clear the windows that were beginning to fog up. "What does that last letter say?"

I slid the letter I'd just read in with the others and opened the last envelope. The return address on this envelope was an apartment on 33rd South—just a few blocks away from the credit union he'd robbed. The message was a quick scrawl, only three sentences with no salutations of any kind—the handwriting shaky.

> *Have the money. If all goes well, will see you tomorrow. If anything happens, talk to Pete.*

It took me a second to understand what I'd just read. I turned to Pete, who was watching me with a strange expression on his face.

"What's it say?" he asked.

I folded the letter slowly, trying to collect my thoughts. A thousand possibilities raced through my mind. "You said you had no idea who my grandfather was talking about."

"So?" His eyes had returned to his driving, darting from the road ahead to his rearview mirror and back.

A question occurred to me that I'd never thought to ask before. "You were a mason, Pete. My grandfather was a carpenter. I guess the two of you must have worked together?"

"A time or two, yeah."

"Were you close?"

"I wouldn't say close. We was neighbors." He glanced down at the sheet of paper in my hands. "What's this all about anyway? What does that letter say?"

"Can you think of any reason why he would have told my grandmother to talk to you?"

"I have no idea what you're talking 'bout." The red circles had returned to Pete's cheeks. His breathing was fast. What was he hiding? Either he was the secret witness my grandfather had written about, or he knew who it was. He'd said that he couldn't read without his glasses. Taking a chance, I held up the letter for him to see.

"My grandfather says right here that you do know. He says that he told you everything."

Pete didn't say a word. He didn't have to. He'd been driving with his left hand on the wheel and his right hand in his coat pocket. Now he pulled the hand from his pocket.

He was gripping a pistol with a barrel that looked at least twelve inches long from where I sat. The bore of the gun stared out like a black, deadly eye.

The black eye was staring at me.

CHAPTER FORTY-THREE

If you've never looked into the barrel of a loaded gun, I don't recommend it. If you have, you know about the numbing fear that turns all of your muscles into limp strands of spaghetti and renders your mind nearly useless. My brain was screaming to my body, *Do something, do something, do something!* But exactly what I was supposed to do was lost in a buzz of static.

"Pete, what are you—" I tried to raise my hand—which felt like it weighed at least fifty pounds—but Pete waved it back down with his gun.

"Give 'em over," he grunted.

His eyes were nothing but slits as he watched me slide the music box and my grandfather's letters across the seat. The veins along his neck bulged and pulsed. Somehow managing to keep the truck on the road while watching me, he reached out with his gun hand and pulled the items onto his lap.

"He lied," Pete growled. "Stewart always was a liar."

"I believe you," I said, my voice sounding tiny and weak. "You can keep the letters. Just put down the gun."

"Told Elsie she never should have married him. Told her she should . . ." His voice died away as he swallowed hard.

I can never keep my big mouth shut when I need to. It's like the circuit that connects my brain to my mouth is on a five-second delay. I remembered the first day I'd seen Pete stopped in front of Gam's house—how he'd said Elsie was pretty as a picture. I blurted out, "You told her she should have what, Pete? Married you instead?"

Pete's face tightened as though he'd been slapped, but the gun never wavered. "You hush up about that," he said. His finger moved on the trigger, and for a moment I pressed up against the door, sure he was going to shoot me. Then he eased off the pressure as he swung the truck into a wide left turn. Looking through the rain-blurred windshield, I realized that we'd just entered the road to his house.

"When people notice I'm gone, they'll come looking for me," I said, trying to keep the fear out of my voice and failing miserably. "They'll know it was you."

"Ain't gonna hurt ya," he said gruffly. His eyes said something else entirely. There was no rage in his expression—only a clear, cold calculation. I knew he was planning on killing me as clearly as if it were printed across his forehead.

There were miles of field on Pete's land where a body could be buried with nobody having a clue. A new thought crossed my mind—one that sent icy tendrils of dread throughout my body. No one had seen me get into Pete's truck. No one—not even Clay—knew where I was.

As we cleared the top of the hill, a bolt of lightening forked down into the valley, illuminating the buildings below with an eerie purple glow. Suddenly I remembered something else—something I should have seen before. Clay had said that his grandfather paid for all of this by selling his property off to vacationers.

That didn't make sense. The date of Pete's barn building in the newspaper article had been 1984, but Echo Lake hadn't become a real tourist destination until the last ten years or so. If the money didn't come from selling vacation property . . . Things began to connect in my mind, pieces I'd had all along but just hadn't put together.

"Pete," I said softly, "how did you pay for your new barn? The one you built the summer after my grandfather was murdered?"

Pete glanced slyly at me as the truck jounced through potholes filled with brown water.

"Think your so smart, don't ya? If you were smart, you'd a left back when I told ya to."

As the truck began to slow, I slid across the seat, feeling for the door handle behind me. My fingers closed on the cool metal. Sensing my intentions, Pete pressed the barrel of his gun against the side of my neck. "Don't make no move 'less I tell ya to."

He pulled the truck around the side of the house—out of sight from anyone who might come up the drive—and turned off the ignition. The only sounds were the rain pelting against the metal roof, the pinging of the truck's engine, and my pulse throbbing in my head. A strong, sudden gust of wind shook the truck, rattling the keys against the steering column.

Pete pushed the letters into the box and tucked it under his left arm. "Stewart was the worst kind of skunk, pure and simple. First he stole Elsie's heart, then he stole that money to try and buy it back."

"And you stole it from him," I finished. "So, what does that make you?"

Pete reached behind himself to open the door and, without a trace of irony, said, "Its rightful owner."

"Follow me out of the truck," he said, keeping the pistol pressed against my neck. "Slowly."

I had no choice but to slide across the seat. As I stepped out the door, the wind nearly knocked me from my feet. Rain slashed diagonally through the air, stabbing my hands and cheeks.

"You don't have to do this," I said. "Whatever happened between you and my grandfather is nobody's business but yours. Just take me back to town, and I promise I'll leave and never come back."

He didn't bother answering. Instead, he moved so that he was standing behind me and, taking a handful of the back of my sweatshirt, marched me around the house and toward the barn. Ducking my head against the downpour, I concentrated on keeping my feet. I was already starting to shiver from the cold, and I got the feeling that if I tripped, he would go ahead and kill me where I lay.

I hoped that the darkened barn might present a chance to escape. But again, the old man seemed to read my thoughts. As we stepped through the doorway, he gave me an unexpected shove in the back, sending me to my hands and knees. "Don't move," he barked.

I cringed, wondering whether I'd hear the report of the gun before I felt the pain of the bullet. Not that it mattered. Instead I heard a metallic rattling, then Pete was back at my side. "On your stomach. Hands behind your back."

I dropped to the barn floor, my face pressed into a mix of hay and dirt that smelled strongly of horses. Pete yanked my right hand painfully up against my back and twisted something around my wrist. It felt like bailing wire. After wrapping my right wrist tightly enough to cut off the circulation, he did the same with my left, leaving my hands pressed against one another, and my arms stretched awkwardly behind me.

Grabbing me by the shoulders, he lifted me to my feet with seemingly little effort. This was not the trembling old man I'd seen the night before. I wondered if he'd been putting on an act for my benefit.

"We're gonna walk apiece," he said. "Don't try nothing, or I'll have to shoot ya."

I didn't bother pointing out that he obviously intended on doing just that anyway.

Back out in the weather, the icy rain quickly soaked through my shirt and jeans. My hair was plastered to my face, and in minutes my teeth began to chatter wildly. I knew that Pete was fine beneath his baseball hat and fleece-lined coat. For some reason that bothered me even worse than the fact that he was planning on killing me.

With each step we took, my anger grew hotter—a seething ball of hot lead in my stomach. I imagined the smug grin on his face as he watched my entire body shaking with the cold. What right did he have to treat me this way? Marching me a like a dumb cow to be slaughtered.

The anger gave me a clarity of thought my fear had been unable to provide. If I was going to escape, it had to be soon. The cold was sapping the energy from my arms and legs, and I couldn't even feel my hands. Another ten minutes of this, and my body would be incapable of acting on any plan my brain might be able to come up with.

As we slogged through the pouring rain, I studied the terrain around us. We were walking roughly parallel to a barbed-wire fence strung along an endless row of posts twenty or so feet to our left. Up ahead to our right, open countryside disappeared into a curtain of darkness and downpour. I'd never be able to escape in that direction. But less than five feet past the fence, a field of corn six feet high stretched as far as I could see. It was my only chance.

I risked a quick glance over my shoulder, judging the distance between Pete and myself. He was walking a step or two behind me, close enough to get off a shot, but still safely out of my reach. My arms and legs were shaking so badly, but his gun hand held steady.

It's got to be now, I told myself. *Whatever you're going to do, do it now.*

Without any warning, I abruptly stopped, bracing my left leg on the wet ground in front of me. Pete started to say something, but there was no time to see whether he'd been able to maintain the distance between us or not. Putting all my weight on my left leg, I raised my right foot and pistoned it back and down. My shoe connected with something solid—the inside of his shin, I hoped—and Pete let out a grunt of pain.

Without looking back, I ran.

CHAPTER FORTY-FOUR

Expecting to feel the hot bite of a bullet hitting my body at any moment, I raced for the fence. Through the drenching rain, it seemed impossibly far away. I could hear Pete screaming, but whether from pain, anger, or both, I had no idea. My legs trembling and slipping on the wet grass, I ran for all I was worth, knowing that with my hands tied behind my back, a trip could cost me my life.

Five feet from the gleaming barbed wire, the sound I'd been expecting came—the sharp crack of a gunshot. With no idea of how close the shot had been, or when the next one might come, I dropped to the ground. Unable to break the fall with my hands, I hit hard, knocking the air from my lungs with a whoosh.

For a moment I could only lie there, trying to catch my breath. A second shot exploded. I dug my feet into the damp earth, searching for any kind of traction, and wriggled toward the fence. Mud went up my nose, in my mouth, and down the front of my shirt. The bottommost strand of barbed wire seemed impossibly close to my face. Pressing my check to the ground, trying not to imagine impaling my skin on its pointed barbs, I slid under the fence.

From behind me came the sound of heavy footsteps pounding across the wet ground. Another explosion—this time I felt the bullet lift the hair from the back of my head.

I was nearly through the fence when the leg of my jeans caught on the barbed wire. Panic flooded my brain as I tried ineffectively to pull free. *Going tharn,* I thought. It was the term the rabbits in *Watership Down* used to describe the debilitating fear of being caught in the farmer's snare. I could hear Pete's voice clearly. "Get back here!" he screamed. "Come back or I'll kill ya."

No. I'm not a rabbit, and I won't go tharn. Forcing myself to think clearly, I slid backward. Instantly my pant leg came free. After pushing the rest of the way under the fence, I got to my feet. Pete fired again. This time the sound of the gunshot was accompanied by a searing pain across my left side.

* * *

Before Pete could get off another round, I disappeared into the maze of corn and out of his sight. Cornstalks sliced at my face and body as I ran heedlessly past them. Several feet into the field I cut right. Twenty more feet and a left. Another left and then a right. I had no idea of where I was going or how close behind Pete might be. The crashing of the rain and my own harsh breathing made it impossible to hear his pursuit.

With each inhalation of air, pain sparked across my side and under my arm. I thought I could feel blood dripping down into the waist of my pants, but rain-soaked as I was, I couldn't tell for sure. At some point the rain turned to hail and now, along with the cutting leaves of the cornstalks, stinging bits of ice struck at every inch of my exposed flesh.

Finally, too exhausted to go any farther, I collapsed to the ground. Gasping for air, I closed my eyes and uttered a short prayer. *Please, Heavenly Father, help me get out of this. Help me get home.*

My arms had gone completely numb up to the elbow. It was strange feeling them pressing against my spine, but unable to feel anything with them—as if they were someone else's limbs. I began to move them back and forth a little, hoping I wasn't digging the bailing wire deeper into my skin, but knowing that if I didn't get the blood flowing back to my hands soon, I wouldn't be able to use them at all.

Around me, the cornstalks whipped to and fro like ghostly specters dancing in the darkness. Pete could be anywhere out there, drawing closer, following my trail of broken plants—even now preparing to take a final, killing shot. I worked harder at moving my hands. Did I feel a slight loosening? It was hard to tell, but I thought one of the strands of wire might have snapped.

I redoubled my efforts, moving my arms up and down as well as side to side. The wires were definitely loosening. Fighting to keep my teeth from chattering audibly, afraid that at any minute I'd see Pete's creased face staring out at me through the darkness, I concentrated on visualizing each wire binding my wrists bending and snapping.

I wasn't even aware that I had finally freed my hands until they dropped to my sides. The wires had cut into each of my wrists, and blood oozed from the cuts. At least the cuts weren't deep. Already the flow of blood was slowing, congealing around the wire.

As if working with a pair of rusty pliers, I slowly forced the fingers of my right hand to close around the exposed end of a broken wire wrapped around my left wrist. At first my wet fingers kept slipping dumbly from the end of the wire or piercing themselves on its jagged tip until I felt like crying out in frustration. But, at last, I was able to twist it off my wrist.

One by one, I wrestled each of the wires from my hands. As the blood rushed back down my arms and into my fingers, a million fiery darts stabbed at every nerve ending, making me cry out with pain against my strongest efforts not to.

Finally, when the terrible burning in my hands had subsided enough that I could bear to move them, I lifted up the side of my soaked sweatshirt. Terrified of what I might see, but even more afraid not to know, I looked down at the spot where I'd been shot.

For a moment I thought I'd pass out—blood seemed to be everywhere. *Don't you faint,* I commanded myself. Looking closer, I realized that lifting my wet sweatshirt had smeared the blood from the wound, making it appear worse then it really was. The bullet had only grazed my ribs. Still, dark drops continued to drip slowly down my side, and watching it seemed to make everything go slightly fuzzy.

I pulled my shirt back down before I could look at it again. For the moment the lightheadedness went away, but I knew it could come back at any minute. Although the hail had stopped, and the rain was dying down, the mountain wind was as ice-cold and strong as ever. If I didn't get somewhere warm soon and find a way to stop my bleeding, I *was* going to pass out. Pete wouldn't need to worry about killing me. The weather would do it for him.

Overhead, the fast-moving thunderheads parted briefly, letting a sliver of silver moonlight peek through. Wrapping my arms around myself, both for warmth and to slow the bleeding, I got to my feet. It didn't make any difference. The tops of the corn, well above my head, whipped wildly back and forth, like a raging sea.

I turned slowly, trying to get my bearings, but there was nothing else to see—no visible landmarks of any kind. Running for my life, I'd lost all sense of direction and between the wind and hail I couldn't even see my own back trail. A hoarse, wracking cough shook my body, tearing at my injured rib. I realized that with no idea which way lead back to the road, even if Pete didn't find me, I really *would* die out here.

Before I could decide which direction to head, a strange, low rumbling sound filled the air. At first I thought it was thunder. But it went on too long and it seemed to be getting closer. Kneeling, I put my hand to the ground. I wasn't sure, but I thought I could feel it shaking slightly.

Again, the feeling of being a trapped rabbit returned. My body began to shake harder than ever, and this time I knew it wasn't just the cold. I stood up on my tiptoes, searching for the source of the sound. It seemed to be coming from off to my right. Then the wind shifted and I could have sworn it was coming from the left. It was growing steadily louder, a deep rattling like a swarm of hornets or a stampede of cattle. In the swirling wind it seemed to be coming from every-where at once.

The thought briefly crossed my mind that this might be someone coming to my rescue. But no one else knew I was here. No one knew where to look for me. And this wasn't the sound of rescue. It was an ominous sound—danger—growing louder by the second. I spun around. *Tharn, tharn, tharn.* The word pounded in my head like a mantra. It was coming. Something bad was coming.

All at once, from off to the right, four bright eyes appeared out of the darkness, and I knew what the sound was. Pete had returned to the barn. He had started up the combine.

He was coming to kill me.

CHAPTER FORTY-FIVE

Transfixed with fear, I watched the machine roar past less than twenty feet to my right. Tires taller than my head churned across the muddy field. Shining metal blades ripped through the corn stalks, leaving a swath of open ground easily fourteen to sixteen feet across. If I was caught in those blades, they'd tear me to pieces. A hundred yards past my hiding place, Pete swung the combine around and disappeared from view.

Where was he? Edging near enough to the sheared stalks to peek out, I quickly glanced in both directions. There was no sign of him—no sign of anything but the dark, rain-swept night. Then I heard it again, the sound of the combine growing louder and louder. Where was it coming from? Backing into the corn, I searched for the glow of the head-lights, but the stalks were too tall.

If I crossed the open rows and the spotlights mounted on the front and back of the cab picked me out, I'd have no chance. The roaring grew until I could actually feel it pounding on my eardrums and vibrating up through the ground into my feet. I had to run. Which way? Blinding light split through the corn. I dove to the ground. Beside me, the blades passed close enough that I could have reached out and touched them.

Again he turned the combine and disappeared from view. This path had crisscrossed the one he'd just made. Was he running some sort of pattern, trying to herd me away from the safety of the barn or crossing the field randomly hoping to force me into a panic?

If that was his plan, it was working. The sound of the combine faded for the moment, but it would be back soon. Arms and legs shaking, I tried to come up with a plan. I could almost feel the energy draining from my body like an overused battery. I had to get to somewhere warm and dry. There was a telephone at the house if I could just reach it while Pete was still in the field. But I head no idea of which direction the house was. If I went the wrong way—

The roaring drew close—deafeningly loud—and I was barely able to slip out of range of the lights before they reached me. Stumbling through the rows of waving plants, I began to run a course angling away from the path Pete was taking.

Every few minutes the combine reappeared—never coming from the same direction—and I had to turn at the last minute to avoid it. In the glare of its lights, I could see how the cornstalks were sucked up into the machine's great maw. Bits of shredded plant shot out of the back in a fountain of dark green. He was getting too close. I'd never be able to make it.

Frightened by the noise, a white rabbit stopped briefly in my path, looked up at me with wide, terrified eyes and then in blind confusion leapt directly toward the path of the combine. *I won't be a rabbit,* I thought.

Ignoring the pain burning in my side and the way my vision was beginning to blur, I ran through the corn, stretching my legs for every extra inch. I couldn't think about what would happen if he found me before I made it back to the house. Lowering my head, I concentrated on putting one foot in front of the other.

Pete roared past, the sound of the combine like the snarl of some prehistoric predator. It was getting closer, and my strength was giving out. I was beginning to falter, my feet catching on the corn stalks or clods of dirt I passed. *Keep going, keep going, keep—*

Without warning I shot out of the corn and onto open ground. Skidding to a stop, I narrowly missed running into another length of barbed-wire fence. For a moment, I thought I'd gone the wrong direction, but then, in the glow of the moon, I saw the barn, and behind it the house. I'd reached the far end of the field. Less than ten feet to my left was the corner where both lengths of fence met.

Dropping to my stomach, I squeezed beneath the bottom strand of the fence, careful to keep the back of my shirt from catching on the barbs. My side screamed in pain as I wriggled across the dirt, but with the sound of the combine growing louder every second, there was no time to think about that.

Once clear of the fence, I got to my feet and started up a steep rise that led to the house. Glancing over my shoulder I saw a dismayingly small amount of corn still standing. If Pete cleared the field before I got out of sight, there would be nowhere left to hide. The lights of the combine were growing brighter. I had to get up the hill before he reached the fence, but the waist-high grass pulled at my exhausted legs.

Turning again, I froze in terror. The spotlights' beams were less than twenty feet behind me, and gaining rapidly. There was no way I could make it to cover without being seen. With nowhere else to go, I dropped into the grass, praying that it was tall enough to hide me.

The lights burned across my hiding place, illuminating every strand of grass in stark detail. It was impossible that Pete could miss me. Pressing my face to the wet earth, I waited for the sound of tearing metal as the combine's blades ripped through the strands of barbed wire. How long would it take him to reach me? Thirty seconds? A minute? In the kind of condition I was in, I wouldn't be able to evade the combine's blades for long.

Then, as if by magic, the lights moved away. The sound of the combine's engine began to fade. Somehow he'd failed to see me. Cautiously, I raised my head from the grass. I halfway expected to see Pete at the fence, waiting to pounce on me. But the combine was going in the other direction, chewing through the last of the corn with eager haste. When he reached the end of that row, Pete would know that I'd escaped, and he'd come looking for me.

Getting to my feet, I tried to run again, but my legs wobbled and threatened to give out. It was all I could do to keep moving steadily up the slope toward the house. If the doors were locked, I'd break a window. It was the first place Pete would look when he realized I'd gotten away, so after I called for help, I'd have to find someplace else to hide. Someplace out of the cold.

At the top of the hill, I headed for the back door of the house. Then I saw something that changed my plans entirely. The door to Pete's truck was still open, and the keys were there. He'd left them hanging from the ignition when he'd pulled me out of the truck.

It was almost too good to be true, and for a moment I sensed a trap. Had he left them for me intentionally, trying to lure me into the truck for some reason? That was stupid. In his agitation, he'd simply forgotten to take them out. In the distance, I could hear the combine drawing closer again, although the barn blocked it from view.

I slid across the cracked plastic upholstery of the truck's seat, pulled the door closed, and turned the key. The engine cranked slowly over, sputtered, and coughed to life. The seat was too far back for me, and I could barely reach the pedals, but there was no time to try and move it. Pete could show up at any second.

Heart pounding, I pressed in the clutch and shoved the gearshift into first. The truck leaped forward and stalled. The seconds were ticking by, and I still had no idea where Pete was. Surely by now he'd realized I was no longer down in the field. Sliding forward so that my rear barely touched the edge of the seat, I started the truck again, this time trying second gear. Miraculously I managed to pull away without stalling this time .

Without turning on the headlights, I edged forward. The ancient pickup had no power steering, and it took all of my strength to turn the big wheel. I could barely see over the dashboard, and without headlights, the road was all but invisible. As I turned onto the muddy road, the tires lost traction and the truck began to slip sideways. I gunned the engine, and the tires caught hold as the truck shot forward.

Afraid that I'd go off the road, I turned on the lights. Immediately the paved surface came into view beneath the tired dual beams. I was going to make it. I was going to get away.

I kept thinking that right up until the combine appeared in front of me.

Pete had turned off the lights and I didn't even realize that he was there until the huge machine roared around from the side of the barn. Churning up onto the road, Pete cut off any chance of escape. The combine's blades filled the road from side to side.

Spinning the wheel, I tried to turn into the field. But the tires hit a ditch, throwing me from the seat, and again the truck stalled. Pete flicked on the spotlights, sending a flash of blinding white through the side window of the truck. The combine's cab towered above me. I reached for the keys, thinking that somehow I still might be able to escape. But they'd fallen from the ignition when I hit the ditch.

I caught a brief glimpse of green-tinted silver as the blades rushed toward me. At the last second, I pushed open the door, and then everything coalesced into a tempest of crushing metal and shattering glass.

The tractor caught the front of the pickup truck, lifting it into the air and spinning it sideways. I had just enough time to think, *This can't be happening* before I was thrown through the door. Behind me, the truck's windshield exploded, showering me with tiny bits of glass.

Bright lights filled the night as the growl of the combine overwhelmed everything. I saw the truck fly through the air like a child's toy. Pressing myself against the cold, wet earth, I buried my head in my hands, and waited for it to crush me.

CHAPTER FORTY-SIX

I'm not good at pain. I never have been. As a kid, I couldn't stand getting shots. The doctor would show me the needle, and I'd belt out a high C that could shatter glass. Afterward, he'd offer a lollipop, like that somehow made it all right. They warn you about strangers offering candy, but personally I've always had a much bigger problem with doctors and sweets.

But nothing I've ever experienced prepared me for the pain of being thrown from a rolling truck into a roadside ditch. One second I was hanging loosely in the air, limbs dangling every which way. The next second, I felt as if a giant fist had crushed me flat.

Streamers of colored light flashed in front of my eyes. My head filled with a crazy, high-pitched ringing. Every square inch of my body sang out in spasms of agony. I gulped, tried to breathe, realized I couldn't, panicked, tried again, and finally managed to suck in a pencil-thin stream of air with a low, shivery moan.

My body felt so cold that for a moment I was sure I must be dying. I shifted slightly, sending daggers of pain up my spine and into my head. Another rainbow-colored flashbulb exploded in my brain and I started to black out. The only thing that kept me from fainting was the intense cold, and a sound that instantly pulled me to my senses. It was the nearby squeak of a door opening, and the clunk of it slamming closed.

"You there, missy?" Pete's voice, steely clear in the sudden quiet was like a slap in the face. Rolling over, I realized that I was lying in a stream of icy rainwater running beside the road. As I pushed myself up, my hands sunk into the muddy soil that had probably saved my life.

"Come on out now," he said, over the sound of scraping metal and the tinkle of glass. A flashlight beam licked at the darkness, flickered, and disappeared.

Edging my head above the side of the ditch, I peeked out onto the road. Metal and glass were strewn everywhere. The cab of the truck was an almost unrecognizable lump, twisted and steaming beneath the front of the combine. If I hadn't fallen out the door, I'd have been crushed inside it.

Pete was kneeling, shining his flashlight into the wreckage. "You inside?" He sounded tired and out of breath. I wished with a vengeance that he'd just give up, while knowing he never would.

Ignoring the pain that coursed through my body, I dropped silently into the ditch. I began to crawl back toward the house, trying my best to stay out of the flesh-numbing water. At first I wasn't sure I'd be able to do it. My arms and legs cried out with every movement, and my ribs felt as if they were tearing apart.

Although the cut on my right arm had broken open and several deep scratches crisscrossed the backs of my hands, miraculously, none of my bones seemed to be broken. As I continued to crawl, the pain in my limbs faded to a more manageable level.

I worked my way a foot at a time along the side of the road, my teeth clenched to keep them from chattering aloud. The sound of groaning metal carried clearly as did Pete's curses as he unsuccessfully searched for me. Venturing a quick glance in that direction, I saw him using some kind of metal bar to pry open the truck's door. It wouldn't be long before he realized I wasn't in the wreckage.

Hunched low, I quickened my pace. At the bottom of the hill, the ditch grew progressively shallower, spreading the water and decreasing my cover. Behind me, the door finally gave way with a hollow, metallic bong. Pete ducked briefly into the opening before bouncing back to his feet. He swung the light in a wide arc, studying the road to either side of the wreckage.

My escape time had just about reached its limit. Less than two inches of dirt remained between the side of the ditch and the surface of the road. If Pete turned his light in my direction now, I'd be clearly visible. With the house still over two hundred yards away, I'd never be able to reach it without being spotted. Directly across the road from me, was the dark cavern of the barn. If I was quiet I might be able to hide inside.

Pete played his flashlight beam out into the field, walking toward the ditch. Had I left any signs there—telling marks of my passage? With no time to think about it, I climbed onto the road. Keeping as low as possible, I scuttled quickly across the wet surface. Past the wreckage, Pete dropped to his haunches, shining his light up and down the ditch. He rose to his feet, turning in my direction, and I broke for the barn.

Darkness enfolded me as I stepped through the doorway. Crouching in the blackness, my shaking body pressed against the solid wood of the barn wall, I looked back to see if Pete had noticed me. He was walking along the edge of the road. With one hand, he swung his light from left to right. The other held a black object that could only be his gun. If he'd seen anything, he gave no sign of it.

I slipped deeper into the barn. As I did, I saw something that caused a glacial fist to wrap around my heart. On the wooden planks of the barn floor—just far enough inside to be on dry ground, but clearly visible by the slanting light of the moon—were several dark drops. Soaking into the hay and dirt, they'd gone from bright red to a dull black, but I knew what they were.

A trail of dripping blood led from the edge of the road to where I now stood.

* * *

There was no time to cover the marks. Pete was nearly even with the barn. If I stepped out into the moonlight now, he'd see me for sure. Holding my hands out in front of me, I moved deeper into the barn. With the far door closed and only the occasional crack in the walls letting in any light at all, I was effectively walking blind.

My fingers brushed against something that jangled in the darkness. I froze, hoping Pete hadn't heard. When he didn't appear in the doorway, I reached carefully forward and touched several lengths of leather hanging from nails on the wall—bridles. The horse stalls, I remembered, were just ahead. On the top of a railing, my groping hands found the coarse surface of a horse blanket. I gratefully wrapped it around me.

The idea of slipping into one of the stalls was tempting. The hay would be warm and dry, but when Pete thought to look in here—which I knew he would—I'd be trapped. Moving past the stalls, I felt my way along stacks of gunnysacks, both empty and full. There had to be something in here I could use for a weapon—a hammer, a scythe, even a length of pipe.

Without warning, a beam of light shot through the darkness as Pete stepped into the doorway.

"You in here, missy?" he called out, his voice echoing in the darkness. Afraid to make a sound, I stood stock still, pressed against the piles of feed.

Pete reached inside the door for something. Too late, it occurred to me that he was about to turn on the lights. There was no place for me to hide. Cringing, I waited for the flood of illumination that would leave me exposed and defenseless. The click of the switch was crystal clear in the stillness. Nothing happened. He flipped more switches. Still no light.

The storm, I realized. *It must have knocked out the power.*

Muttering something unintelligible, Pete fiddled with the lights a few more times before finally giving up. Silhouetted in the moonlight, he peered into the interior of the barn as if trying to make up his mind whether to continue his search inside or go back out. His flashlight crisscrossed the bales of hay and rows of heavy equipment, its beam swallowed by the immensity of the large, dark building.

Motionless, I willed myself into invisibility. The circle of light played across the horse stalls, the light switches, then stopped on the floor. Had he seen the blood? In the dim light, I couldn't tell whether he was actually looking down or just letting the flashlight hang at his side. *Let him go away,* I prayed. *Let him leave me alone.*

As if he'd heard my prayer, Pete turned around. He stepped out through the doorway, and a thousand pound weight slipped from the back of my neck. Now if only I could find a weapon of my own or some kind of—

The sound of scraping across the ground outside froze me in place. The square of moonlight at the front of the barn began to disappear and, without warning, Pete was back. He was pulling the barn door closed. Just before it rolled shut, he stepped inside.

"Fun and games is over," he said, his voice low and grave. "It's time to put an end to this business once and for all."

CHAPTER FORTY-SEVEN

"Ain't no way out of here now. The other door's locked, and I ain't letting you outa this one." With the barn door closed and the rain stopped, Pete's voice carried clearly through the large open space.

He stepped forward, swinging his gun around as if expecting an ambush. "You can make this easy, or you can make this hard," he drawled. "Either way, it's gonna end the same."

It was crazy, but a part of me—the trembling rabbit part—wanted to step out into the open with my hands raised and just get it over with. My strength was all but gone, and now my only chance for escape was to somehow wrestle Pete's gun away from him.

Standing in the middle of the barn, so that he could reach both sides with his light, he began inching forward a step at a time.

"Guess you wonder how I done it?" he said. "Got away with killing your granddad for all these years." He moved closer, crouching down to let the light shine between the treads of the caterpillar combine to his left.

"'Twasn't that hard," he said, cackling softly.

What little adjustment my eyes had made to the darkness had been ruined by Pete's light. Trying to time my steps with his, I slipped backward, running my hand along the stack of bags to my left. Each step risked the chance of running into something that might give away my presence, but it was either that or wait for him to find me.

"After nearly twenty years, Stewart phones me one day out of the blue. Well, you can imagine my surprise. He asks me if I would talk to Elsie for him. Tell her he didn't never touch his daughter and ask her to take him back.

"'Course I said no. Weren't no way I'd help an egg-sucking dog like him. He never deserved a woman like Elsie in the first place, and I knew she'd never take him back no matter what I or anyone else said."

Pete moved with a steady, robot-like consistency. Forward a step, scan left and right—taking the time to search any space or cubby where I might be hiding—and forward again. All the while keeping up his running dialogue as though trying to lull me to sleep.

"That's when he mentioned the money. Said he knew a way to get his hands on over four hundred thousand dollars. Figured it was stolen, but I got to thinking. Times was tough then, and a lot of folks was selling their land dirt cheap. Fellah with some brains could do right smart for his self if he had that kinda cash.

"I told him I might be able to help him some. Said I knew a fellah who seen the whole thing. Told him he might be willing to talk to Elsie for the right price."

By now I had nearly reached the far end of the barn without finding anywhere to hide or anything I could use as a weapon. It was as if Pete had intentionally removed everything that might be able to help me. I could feel despair sucking the air from my lungs, sapping the last of the energy from my body.

"Old fool agreed to come to my house with the cash. I figured I could take the money, pretend to talk to Elsie, and send him on his way." Pete checked each of the stalls. "Musta got his wind up though," he said, coughing at the clouds of chaff his boots had kicked up. "Went to Elsie's house 'stead of coming to me."

Moving backward, I walked straight into a wooden beam that seemed to rattle all the way up to the roof of the barn. Pete was out of the stall like a cat, waving his light wildly. "I hear you," he cackled. " Come out, come out wherever you are. Olly, olly oxen free!"

I dropped to my knees behind the beam, paralyzed with fear.

Pete stared into the darkness, head cocked like a barn owl listening for the footsteps of a mouse. When, after several minutes, I hadn't moved, he lowered the flashlight and continued on with his search.

Rising from my hiding place, I wrapped my arms around the beam and realized there was not one beam but two, both attached to the floor and rising into the darkness. Nailed between them was a short length of board, and a little higher up, another. Running my hands across the wood, I realized what it was—a ladder, leading up into the hayloft.

I placed one foot on the first rung and paused. Was this the right thing to do? I'd be just as trapped above as I was below—even more so. And once I committed myself, there'd be no turning back. Still, the end of the barn was close now. I could see a few tentative rays of moonlight shining through the cracks.

Although my eyes hadn't completely adjusted to the darkness, I could see that the stack of bags I'd been following continued all the way to the end of the wall. It was a dead end. With fewer hiding places to explore, Pete was moving more quickly now. The longer I waited, the greater the chance he'd spot me before I reached the top of the ladder. Praying the boards wouldn't creak under my weight, I reached for the next rung up and began to climb.

The sensation of trusting my life to a ladder I couldn't see was more than a little unsettling. Although I knew that both the top and bottom of the ladder were secured, it was easy to imagine one of the rungs hanging loosely by a single rusted nail. Just as I placed my weight on it, the board would give way, sending me catapulting through the air to the hard wood below.

Glancing down, I was amazed at how high I'd climbed. Pete's beam sweeping slowly from side to side was easily twenty or thirty feet below. And yet, he had nearly reached the base of the ladder. It would be an easy matter to pick me off if he looked up while I was still on it. Trying to ignore the aching in my arms and the burning pain in my side, I pushed myself to climb more quickly.

At the top of the ladder, I reached for the next board— shifting my foot from one rung to another as I stretched up—and grabbed a handful of nothing. One minute I was tightly anchored to the ladder, and the next I was tilting backward, all balance lost. Unable to help myself, I cried out in fear and surprise.

Flailing with my free arm, I just managed to hook the edge of the loft. Below me, I heard Pete shout. His light swung up to where I was. Without bothering to look down, I pulled myself the rest of the way through the opening and climbed out onto the piled hay.

"Got you now!" Pete screamed, his voice echoing through the rafters. "I've got you now."

Pressing my face into the soft hay, fragrant with the aroma of broad fields and open air, I gasped for breath, my heart fluttering wildly. It *had* been a mistake to come up here. Now, with no way out, I was trapped.

I could feel the floor beneath me vibrate as Pete climbed onto the ladder. Panicked, I crawled through the hay—no longer thinking rationally, only trying mindlessly to get away.

"I can hear you creepin' about," Pete called, "scurrying like a scared little mousie. It's almost over." Pete's voice was closer. He sounded winded but insanely cheerful.

Mindless with terror, I nearly crawled across a long, wooden handle without stopping. Another foot or two to the left or right and I'd have missed it entirely. Only when my kneecap came directly down on its hard round surface, did I realize something was buried beneath the hay.

Backing up, I caught hold of the handle and ran my hand down its splintery length. At the end was a cross bar with five curved metal prongs. I couldn't see it, but in my mind, I could picture what I was gripping.

It was a pitchfork.

CHAPTER FORTY-EIGHT

Pete was just out of sight. Standing on the ladder, but unsure of where I was, he waited. I could hear his breath, see the flicker of his light turning the straw around me to gold.

"I know you're there," he rasped. He reached tentatively through the opening with his flashlight, daring me to move.

I didn't bite.

The light disappeared back out of sight.

In and out his breath went, each gasp labored and uneven. He *was* an old man after all, and the running and climbing had worn on him.

"Didn't plan on killin' Stewart," he said, after a moment. "I seen his truck parked out front of Elsie's place, an' figured he was up to no good. I went inside and we . . ."

Pete's voice faded away, the silence stretching out so long I began to sense a trick. What was he doing down there? Holding tight to the pitchfork, I tensed, waiting for him to burst into view. Then he spoke again, his voice hoarse with emotion, and I realized he was crying.

"When you said I loved Elsie . . . I guess you was right. My Janey was only twenty-four when she died giving birth to our only child, and I just sorta figured that Elsie and I would end up together."

The ladder creaked a little as Pete shifted his weight. "When Stewart told me he was back for good—whether Elsie liked it or not—I guess I went a little crazy. I pushed him, and he fell. Hit his head on the corner of the wall. Next thing I know, he's running up the stairs, and I'm chasing him with a stick of firewood. Then he's laying on the ground an' I'm standing over him . . . An' he's dead."

So that was what it had come down to. A simple case of jealousy—probably the most common reason in the world for murder. Only what Pete called love was really selfishness. He wanted my grandmother the same way he'd wanted the money. And he was willing to do whatever it took to get what he wanted.

"After that, everything happened purty quick. Elsie come in the house. I couldn't let her know what I'd done. So I said I seen Trevor run out of the house with a bloody club. He was around her place a lot. Fellah was a little slow, and I didn't figure it'd be too hard to throw the blame on him." Pete chuckled, a sound both sardonic and creepy—the kind of laughter you might expect to hear from a disturbed little boy, just before he killed a small animal.

"Didn't count on her having feelings for the moron. When she seen Stewart's body, she went on and on 'bout how it was all her fault, and how she couldn't let Trevor go to jail. Then she did the golldarndest thing. Said if there wasn't no witnesses, they couldn't throw Trevor in jail. Said she was leaving town and made me swear not to tell a soul what I seen."

Pete continued with the rest of his story. But there was no need. Trevor's actions—the account he stuck to in jail, even though Gam was dead—suddenly made tragically logical sense. When Gam left, Pete had seen a way to use their feelings for each other to create the perfect cover.

He tracked down Trevor and told him that Stewart had come back to town, and Elsie had killed him. He explained how she had left town to avoid arrest. Had it been hard to convince the poor muddled man that the only way to protect his beloved Elsie was to remain silent? To keep vigil over her house?

Trevor had probably assumed that it was only a matter of time before someone realized Stewart was missing. Had he decided even back then, that when the body was finally discovered, he would take the blame? I found the idea all too plausible.

Trevor and my grandmother were scared to death to contact one another, knowing that legally they could be forced to testify against each other. Knowing what was in the house, they'd each felt tied to the building without ever daring to enter. And so, like two lovers destined by fate to remain forever apart, they had each waited for my grandfather's body to be discovered.

Only it never had been found. With the money from the bank robbery, Pete had no reason to say a word. Trevor had kept watch over Gam's house for all of these years, scaring away any trespassers who might get too near it. And what about Gam? How she must have watched the papers— waited for the phone call to say that her husband's body had been found. It must have driven her nearly crazy.

It had driven Trevor to drink.

If Pete's story had been designed to catch me off guard, his ruse worked. While my mind was caught up in a murder committed twenty years earlier, he slipped quietly up into the loft. I didn't even know he was there until the beam of his flashlight blinded me with its brightness.

He'd have killed me on the spot if he'd seen me. But maybe I'd been just a little bit smarter than he expected as well. As he'd climbed the ladder, I'd buried myself in the bed of soft hay—close enough to strike, but hidden from view. He stood only a few feet away from me—gun in hand— but the beam from his flashlight slipped harmlessly across my hiding place.

Not moving a muscle, almost afraid to breath, I watched him turn a quick, confused circle. No doubt he'd expected to find me huddling in a corner, waiting for the bullet that would kill me and protect his secret.

But I had another idea in mind. Tensing, I willed him to draw just a step closer. I had to hurt him, to stop him once and for all. Clenching my damp fists around the handle of the pitchfork, I knew I'd only get one chance. I wanted to make it count.

He began to move in my direction—hesitated—turned halfway to his left, tilting his head as though listening for the sound of my frightened breathing, the freight-train pounding of my pulse. For the moment, his gun hung slightly downward, pointed at the floor. *Come on,* I silently pleaded, *just one step closer.*

Gathering my legs beneath me, I pressed my feet against the floor of the loft. Whether he stepped toward me or away, I had to take advantage of his confusion now. I couldn't give him any more time to figure out what I was up to.

He swung his head around, the light shining off to my right, and took a hesitant step in that direction. Bringing the pitchfork even with my face I prepared to spring.

And then everything went wrong.

* * *

Just as I rose up from the hay, a sharp buzzing sound filled the barn. Without warning, every light in the building came on as the electricity was restored. Pete spun in my direction, his old blue eyes widening as he saw what I was holding.

Before he could get off a shot, I lunged forward. I was aiming the pitchfork dead center of his chest. But at the last second, my feet slipped in the hay, and my arm went left. Pete saw me coming but didn't have time to move. The best he could do was raise his arm holding the flashlight.

The metal tines of the fork ripped through the cloth of his shirt, stabbing his arm. With an expression of pained surprise he looked at his arm. "Gah," he mouthed, his jaw dropping open.

The flashlight he'd been holding in his left hand fell to the floor with a muted clunk. But the gun was in his right hand. Recovering quickly he brought it up. My only chance was to keep him from getting off a shot. I dove for his gun, closing one hand around the barrel and the other around his right wrist. Pete managed to squeeze the trigger, but the bullet entered harmlessly into the floor.

Instantly, the gun grew hot beneath my fingers. I didn't let go. Ignoring the pain, I slid my other hand from his wrist to the handle of his pistol and twisted. He was bigger and stronger than me, but while I used both hands to wrestle away the gun, his left arm hung uselessly at his side.

Even then, he might have managed to hang on to the gun anyway. I'd gained the initial advantage of surprise, but he was recovering quickly. Just as I felt the handle begin to slide out of his fingers, he brought his elbow hard up under my chin. My head rocked backward, my teeth snapping shut on my tongue.

His fingers tightened, and I knew that I wouldn't be able to outwrestle him with brute strength. Applying the trick I'd used to get away from him in the field, I brought my right foot inside his left leg and stamped down on the inside of his shin with all my strength. Immediately, he collapsed to ground and the gun flew from his hand.

For a second, too surprised by my success to move, I stood staring at the spot where the gun had disappeared into the hay. Then I was on my hands on knees searching for it. Behind me, Pete let out a grunt of pain. I turned just in time to see him pull the pitchfork from his arm with his right hand.

Frantic, I ran my hands through the pile of straw in front of me. The gun couldn't have gone far and yet I couldn't feel it anywhere. Pete stepped toward me, holding the pitchfork in his right hand like a javelin. Just as he brought it down, I rolled to the side. Before I could get up, he was on me. With both hands, I pushed at the handle of the pitchfork, but Pete was heavier and had the advantage of being above me.

Inch by inch, the sharp metal points drew nearer and nearer to my face. I tried to stop him, but my trembling arms were no match for his strength. At the last minute I turned my head and closed my eyes.

"What's going on here?"

I opened my eyes. Clay was standing on the ladder, halfway into the loft. One hand held the side of the ladder.

The other held his service pistol.

Pete drew back the pitchfork. I rolled from beneath him and crawled madly to Clay's side.

"He's trying to kill me. He's got a gun. Somewhere in the hay. He tied my hands. Tried to run me over with the combine." The words spilled from my mouth like water from a fountain. I couldn't seem to stop talking or stop trembling.

"Granddad, is that true?" Clay held his gun aimed slightly toward the ground, halfway between his grandfather and me.

Pete slowly let the pitchfork fall from his fingers.

Clay turned to me. "How did all this happen?"

"I found some letters in my grandmother's music box. They were from my grandfather. They were about Pete. My car wouldn't start, and he was giving me a ride to the mechanic." Suddenly I found that I couldn't speak anymore. Relief at finally being safe dissolved into uncontrollable tears. I clung to Clay's arm like a life preserver.

"It's okay," he said, running a hand across my matted hair. "Everything's going to be fine."

He climbed the rest of the way up the ladder, taking his arm from my hand. "This will all be over soon."

Soon? Something in Clay's voice was wrong. I looked up.

Clay was staring down at me with a look I didn't understand. And despite the blood soaking his shirtsleeve, Pete was grinning. Clamping a hand to his injured arm, he watched with avid interest.

"I'm so sorry you've had to endure all of this," Clay said, his voice cold and emotionless, "but in just a second the pain will be over."

Slowly he raised his gun and pointed it at my head.

CHAPTER FORTY-NINE

"What are you doing?" Was this some kind of sick joke? Clay wasn't smiling.

Swiveling his gun to track me as I rose unsteadily to my feet, he grimaced and shook his head. "I was really hoping it wouldn't come to this."

Pete circled around behind his grandson, blood oozing between his fingers and down his arm. I backed away. Clay didn't bother to follow. There was no place for me to go. "Why are you protecting him? He's a murderer."

"If you'd left well enough alone, everything would have been fine. But you just kept digging." Clay gave me a reproachful glare, as if this were somehow my fault.

I didn't understand. How could I have been so wrong about him? Only the day before he'd saved my life by pulling me out of the fire. Why did he do that if . . . Reality hit so hard, it was like a physical blow to the head.

"You did it. You're the one who burned Gam's house."

Clay averted his eyes.

"Torrance thought his money was inside, and Trevor had no reason to do it. Bobby told you I was inside Gam's house, and you burned it down anyway." I hadn't thought my pain could get any worse tonight, but this hurt more than all of my physical injuries. "You let me think that you'd saved my life, when really you almost killed me. Why? Why would you do that?"

It was Pete who answered. "Couldn't let you find them papers," he said, his voice calm, as if he was clarifying the evening's weather forecast. "Before your grandfather died, he told me 'bout the letters he sent Elsie. I never knew where she'd put 'em—or if she'd kept 'em at all. She never put two an' two together, but someone else might've."

"You couldn't move the body because that was what kept Gam and Trevor from comparing notes." I continued backing away. "And you couldn't search for the letters without raising suspicions."

Pete nodded. "Shoulda burned the place down soon as Elsie died. But I never could bring myself ta do it."

Clay ran the fingers of his left hand through his hair. "I thought you'd smell the smoke right away and get out. When the window exploded, I realized you were in trouble, and I . . . went in to get you."

"But why? Why go to all that trouble when you could have just let me die?" This was all like some kind of crazy, mixed-up dream.

Clay looked down, tugging at the collar of his shirt with the hand that wasn't holding the gun. Then, unbelievably, he smiled—the same innocent grin that had won me over at the diner. "I thought you knew," he said. "I care for you—a lot. I might have even loved you."

And there it was, his grandfather all over again. He probably couldn't even see the irony in his words. "You don't have any idea what *love* is. You think that because you *want* someone that you *care* for them. You're so selfish that you've actually convinced yourself it's something to be proud of."

He shook his head, managing to look wounded and indignant. "You don't understand."

"I'm beginning to." Unfortunately it was coming a little too late to do any good. "Have you known all along?"

The cold calculation I'd seen in Pete earlier now slipped across Clay's face. I wondered if they knew how much they looked alike, and why I hadn't noticed it before. "Not until the detective called from Salt Lake."

"Did your grandfather kill him, too? Or was that you?"

Clay's pink cheeks darkened. "Enough talking," Pete said. "I told ya—she knows too much. Now let's get this over with so I can take care of my arm."

I had backed nearly to the wall. Behind me was the door where hay was loaded up into the loft. Outside, the clouds had broken, and the dark cover of night was pierced by thousands of twinkling stars.

"It's over thirty feet down," Clay said. "Even if the fall didn't kill you, I'd just have to come down and finish you off. It'll be easier this way."

"You're a police officer. You're supposed to protect people."

"What do you think I'm doing?" he said, glancing toward Pete. "He's the only family I have. I'd think that you of all people should understand the importance of family."

"This isn't about family. Let's at least get that much straight. This is about greed, plain and simple." I didn't want to die, but I wasn't going to grovel either.

"You don't care about your grandfather. All you see is his house, his money, and his property. You see what your grandfather has, and you want it for yourself. That's why Pete killed my grandfather. It's why you're killing me."

Clay looked like he'd been slapped. His face tightened, lips stretched white over his teeth. "That money was never Stewart's anyway. Granddad was only taking money from a thief. "

I was standing at the door of the hayloft. Cold air blew against my neck and cheeks. There was nowhere else to go. "It wasn't just about the money for him. It was about my grandmother. He wanted her, and she wouldn't have him. She wouldn't give you the time of day, would she, Pete?"

Now it was Pete's face that tightened—his color high and hot. "Shoot her," he said, through clenched teeth.

"You know, there's one last thing I've been wondering about," I said. "My grandfather never denied hitting Gam or my mother. But he swore he never molested my mother. Why do you think that is?"

Clay looked nonplussed, but Pete eye's narrowed to wrinkled slits, his jaws clenched and unclenched. I was right.

"It was you, wasn't it? You attacked her that night. You couldn't get to my grandmother so you attacked my mother instead?"

Clay turned to his grandfather. I took the chance to look quickly over my shoulder. The height made my stomach do cartwheels. But on the other side of the road was the trailer full of steer manure I'd noticed earlier in the day. It was a good fifteen to twenty feet away from the barn. Still . . .

Pete laughed, the unexpected noise frightening a pair of swallows from their roosts. Through the narrowed slits of wrinkled skin, his eyes gleamed. A fleck of white spittle clung to the corner of his mouth.

"Wasn't your mother I wanted. It was Elsie. And setting up Stewart was easy as that." He snapped two callused fingers together. "Only had to ask the fool to stay late on a job we was working together. When I seen Trinity coming home, I dragged her inside the house."

"It was night, so she couldn't see you." I walked directly at Pete. "That was brave, picking on a defenseless little girl." Pete's right hand opened and closed, making a fist over and over.

"And when my grandfather came home, you managed to shift the blame to him somehow. You're good at shifting blame, aren't you?" Pete's face had gone nearly purple. A thick vein, like a night crawler writhing across his forehead, pulsed in and out.

"I'm not the one who beat his wife and daughter," Pete shouted. "I never even hurt the girl. Just pulled her around some. Ripped her dress so people would think—"

"Would think my grandfather was a child molester." I was directly in front of him, his hot, sour breath enveloping my face like a rancid cloud. "You ruined his life. You tried to ruin my grandmother's life. And what do you think it did to my mother believing that her father had attacked her? You're not strong, and you're not brave. You're a weak, greedy, pathetic excuse for a human being, and your grandson is no different."

"Shoot her!" Pete howled. "Give me the gun, and I'll do it myself."

Reaching out with his right hand, he snatched the gun away from Clay. It was the only chance I'd have. Without a pause, I turned and ran.

It was less than a dozen steps to the door. If I slipped on the hay or didn't get up enough speed before I jumped, I'd land broken on the ground or crash into the metal side of the trailer. But there was no time to think about that—no time to think about anything. I could only launch myself into the night and let everything else take care of itself.

CHAPTER FIFTY

I've always imagined that the final fleeting seconds of my life will be somehow magical—bright lights at the end of a long tunnel, friends and family pressing forward to greet me, a mini-highlight reel of my life run in full 3-D Technicolor. At the very least, I'd like a moment of reflection to look back on things and say, *I have run the good race.* Is that really too much to ask?

Maybe you have to have a little something prepared in advance, like when you're unexpectedly called upon to speak in Relief Society and you've just read the perfect story in the *Ensign.* Or maybe, instinctively I knew that this wasn't really the end.

I'd like to think that was the case. Otherwise, based on my firsthand experience of flying through the air and into a trailer full of manure, I'd have to say that the whole dying thing has been vastly overrated.

The only thought I had as I fell through the darkness was that Gam's worst nightmare had come true. I was going to die and I was not wearing clean socks.

I think I might also have briefly wondered whether they had all-you-can-eat in heaven. But that might just be my stomach talking. Then I dropped unceremoniously into the middle of the nastiest substance since my experience with the broken sewer pipe.

I'd like to be able to paint a clear, concise picture of what happened after I jumped from the loft. A reporter is trained to take confusing—and at times conflicting—bits of information, sort them out, and present a narrative that is both rational and comprehensive. Unfortunately memories tend to take on a strange taffy-like consistency.

Some parts of what happened—like the sick, out of control spinning sensation I felt in my stomach as the trailer rushed up to meet me—will stay locked in my mind forever. Other parts run together, draw out into extended slow motion sequences that I know can't be right, or have disappeared altogether.

Hitting the mound of cow manure knocked the wind, and what minimal energy reserves I still held, right out of me. I remember lying in the stink, my chest burning as I struggled to take a breath. Every part of my body felt temporarily numb, as if I'd been shot up with a major overdose of Novocain.

The sound of Clay and Pete shouting at each other floated down from the barn. I barely had the strength to turn my head. Clay's silhouette appeared briefly in the hayloft door then slipped from sight.

What was the purpose of all this? I thought. It wouldn't take him more than a few minutes to climb down the ladder, and then I would die just as surely as I would have if I'd stayed up in the barn. All I could do was lie and wait for the inevitable to happen.

The clomp, clomp, clomp of Clay's boots echoed off the rungs as he hurried down. *No need to rush,* I thought. *I'm not going anywhere.* Somewhere in the distance, I heard the roar of an engine. *It's the combine. He's going to kill me with the combine after all.* The thought held less terror than I thought it would. Things going on around me were starting to feel . . . less important.

In the night sky, stars spun lazily overhead. If I had to die, taking my last few breaths under a million tiny suns wasn't a bad way to go. It made up—at least a little bit—for where I was. Flashing lights bounced off the edge of the trailer as voices shouted. I remember wishing that they would turn off the lights and be quiet so I could die in peace.

I thought I heard someone calling my name.

Clay? It didn't sound like Clay. It sounded like . . . Feeling came back to my limbs with an agonizing flow of pain. I'd landed feet first in the trailer—leaning forward a little, like a parody of a ski jumper. My legs were buried almost to the thighs in cow dung, my arms hidden to the elbows.

Pulling my arms from the muck, I managed to drag myself close enough to the edge of the trailer to peer over the side. Pain lanced up my side as I willed myself to do it.

For a moment, what I saw didn't make any sense. Clay was standing near the far corner of the barn, washed in a bright circle of light. He'd taken his gun from Pete, but he was holding it barrel first, away from his body.

"Drop your weapon!" An electronically amplified voice called out.

The voice and the light were coming from a patrol car parked midway between the trailer and me. It sounded like Sheriff Orr. But what was he doing here? Someone else was standing in the dark beside the car. He was crouched near the door.

The figure moved slightly forward so that the brightness from the spotlight illuminated his features, and a million emotions raced through me. It was Bobby—*my* Bobby. Dressed in his dark blue police uniform, he edged toward Clay, his weapon held out in front of him.

"Drop it," he shouted. "Drop it, or I'll shoot."

Clay let the gun fall from his fingers. It hit the earth with a wet thud. Sheriff Orr stepped from the car. He too was holding his gun out in front of him.

"On the ground," he said. "Arms spread."

As Clay dropped face first into the mud, Bobby darted forward and picked up the gun Clay had dropped.

Even as I saw them both standing there, I couldn't convince myself that what I was seeing was actually real. Bobby couldn't possibly be here. He should be in Salt Lake. And the sheriff had no way of knowing I was with Pete.

I tried to call out, but I couldn't seem to draw in enough breath. My lungs wouldn't expand.

Sheriff Orr knelt at Clay's side and snapped a pair of handcuffs closed on Clay's wrists.

"Where is she?" Bobby shouted at him. "Where's Shandra?"

"Here," I called out. "I'm here." But the only sound that came out was a thin whisper I could barely hear myself.

"If you've done anything to her, I'll kill you." Bobby, who wouldn't hurt a fly, sounded tougher than I'd ever heard him. It really *was* Bobby, though. I wasn't imagining it. Somehow he'd known I was in trouble. Somehow he'd come to my rescue.

So why did I still feel scared? Why were alarm bells going off in my head?

Something moved in the darkness. Looking down, I saw a figure slip around the edge of the trailer. It was Pete—and he was holding a gun. He must have found his pistol in the hay while Clay was climbing down the ladder.

"Look out!" I tried to scream. But I couldn't—nothing would come out. Pete slipped noiselessly along the edge of the trailer. He was right below me. If I didn't do something, he'd be able to ambush Bobby and the sheriff while they concentrated on Clay.

Pulling on the edge of the trailer, kicking my feet out of the gunk they were encased in, I managed to break free. Fighting against the blinding pain in my ribs, I climbed over the side. Pete looked up at the last second, but by then I was falling down on top of him.

Someone screamed. The hot explosion of a gunshot came from nearby. The sound of running feet. People calling my name. Light shining in my eyes. None of it seemed to matter to me anymore. I was slipping into a cocoon where pain and cold were far, far away.

Arms wrapped around me, and I was lifted into the air. So familiar, the way these arms cradled me. The rough calloused fingers on my arms. These were the arms that had carried me out of Gam's house, out of the fire. I was sure of it. But Clay was the one who rescued me from fire. He was the one he carried me out. *Wasn't he?*

I opened my eyes, and a face smiled down at me. Tears were shining in his eyes. "Gonna be a'right," he said. His words slurring together as though his mouth was filled with peanut butter and jelly.

It was Trevor.

CHAPTER FIFTY-ONE

"Touch me with that ice-cold torture device, and I'll break every bone in your hand."

Dr. Tae looked from me to his stethoscope and back again.

"I'd listen to her," Bobby said. "She's in one of her moods."

"You'd be in a mood too if you had to eat this gruel." I pushed aside a bowl of some grayish slop that tasted like watered down tile grout and stared morosely at a banana with more bruises than me.

"Maybe I'll just check back in later." Dr. Tae slipped out the door, throwing an uneasy glance at me over his shoulder. I noticed him warming his stethoscope between his hands as he went.

"Do you always talk that way to doctors who save your life?" Bobby was leaning against the windowsll, arms crossed over his chest. A tiny grin played at the corners of his lips.

"I can't help it," I grumped. "I'm starving." He was right, and we both knew it. It wasn't like Pete's bullet had grazed my heart or anything. But three fractured ribs, a gash on my side that required nineteen stitches, two sprained wrists, and a collapsed lung were nothing to sniff at. Not to mention being a hair's breadth away from hypothermia. But I was so-o-o hungry.

"If you could just run down to Mike's and get me a burger with the works and fries, oh and a slice of apple pie—with ice cream—and one of those—"

"La, la, la, la-a-a-a." Bobby put his hands over his ears, singing like a loon until he was sure I'd quit begging. "Even if *you're* not going to listen to your doctors, *I* am."

"Whatever." I peeled open the banana and broke off highly unsatisfying chunks of the mushy fruit.

After I'd finished eating, Bobby pushed himself off the windowsill and came to the side of my bed. "So? Aren't you going to ask how I knew you were in trouble?"

"Nah," I said, feigning indifference. "I'll just read about it in the paper."

I was dying to know, and he was dying even more to tell me. But it was a little game we played, seeing who could get the upper hand. I might be stuck in a hospital bed with lousy food, but I could still make him squirm.

When I felt like he'd suffered enough, I stifled a yawn. "Well, all right. If you've got nothing better to do. You might as well go ahead and tell me."

Bobby checked his watch. "I should probably be getting over to the sheriff's office to see if they need me to fill out any more paperwork."

He was good. But I knew his weaknesses. "Another ten minutes or so and the nurse will be around to take my . . . *blood*." Bobby hates the sight of blood, which is actually pretty funny coming from a cop.

"Fine." He gave a slight shudder, hooked his foot around a chair leg and slid it over. "I first knew something was up when I talked to Sheriff Orr about the body."

"The second one? Detective Harding?"

"Right."

He sat down and we leaned conspiratorially toward each other like a couple of kids telling secrets in the schoolyard. We both love the juicy stuff; it's what made him a cop and me a reporter.

"Two things bothered me about that. First, Detective Harding wasn't killed with your grandmother's music box; the medical examiner was able to determine that easily. So why go to all the trouble of making it look like he was?"

"To frame me." That much was obvious.

"True. But unless the murderer was a complete idiot, he had to know that the police would figure out you didn't kill Harding. Which leads to the second point—the foot-prints."

"Yes, the footprints." With everything that had happened, I'd nearly forgotten about the single set of foot-prints leading up to Gam's room. "How *did* he manage that?"

Bobby leaned back in his chair, checking his watch. "You know I really need to be—"

I grabbed his arms, my wrists throbbing in protest. "Oh-h-h, I *hate* you. Tell me right now, or I'll tell everyone in your precinct about the time you tried to kiss Sally Etterman in the dark and accidentally kissed her brother."

Bobby just grinned. It was a hollow bluff. We both had too many skeletons in the closet to threaten to tell each other's secrets.

"Okay, you win. *Please* tell me how he did it."

Bobby twisted the end of an imaginary mustache. "The first rule of good detective work. 'When you have eliminated the impossible, whatever remains—'"

"'However improbable, must be the truth.' Yeah, yeah, Sherlock, out with it." He was just showing off now, and I was getting cranky again.

"All right. We know that the detective didn't kill himself; the real murder weapon was the pipe Clay planted in Torrance's motel room. Therefore, someone else was in your grandmother's room with Harding."

"There were no other footprints. Harding climbed the stairs by himself."

Bobby grinned smugly. "Unless he never climbed the stairs at all."

"How would Harding get in my grandmother's bedroom without going up the stairs?"

"Oh, he went up the stairs all right. He just didn't *climb* them."

He was waiting for me to figure it out on my own, but I was either too dumb or too tired. I shook my head.

"He was *carried* up."

I sat back against the pillows. "I don't understand. I thought the footprints matched Harding's shoes."

"They did. But Harding wasn't wearing them, Clay was. My theory is that Clay found the detective snooping around the house and hit him over the head with the pipe. He removed Harding's shoes and slipped them onto his own feet instead. Wearing the detective's shoes, he carried him up to your grandmother's bedroom. Maybe he wrapped a towel around Harding's head to keep him from dripping blood along the way. He laid Harding on the floor to bleed to death, put his shoes back on him, and carried your grandfather's body down the stairs, out the front door, and into the cellar."

This all sounded fine except for one vital flaw. "So how does the killer manage to get back down the stairs without leaving any footprints—levitation?"

"Nope," Bobby said, obviously enjoying himself. "In his stocking feet, he tiptoes back down the stairs, staying inside the footprints he made on the way up. It probably wouldn't have passed a real forensics examination, but he knew he'd be able to cover up any mistakes when he and the sheriff came in the next day, and ultimately the fire destroyed everything."

"So the fire wasn't just to destroy the letters, but also to destroy any evidence he might have left."

Bobby nodded. "Once he started the fire, he drove back toward town, waited a few minutes, and then radioed for the fire department."

It was so simple I couldn't believe I hadn't thought of it myself.

"And you figured this all on your own?"

Bobby nodded self-importantly.

"Well, I have to say, I'm impressed."

"That's why they call me McGruff the Crime Dog," he said, polishing his badge with one sleeve.

More like McDuff the Swollen Ego. But that was all right. I gave him his moment of glory. He'd earned it. "What I don't understand is why he and Pete went to all that trouble if they knew I would be cleared anyway?"

Bobby grew serious. "That's what made me suspicious. Whoever set you up knew you'd already been to your grandmother's house. The only people you mentioned seeing were Pete and Clay. And the only reason I could think of for such an elaborate hoax was to get you thrown in jail."

Once the pieces were laid out so clearly, everything made much more sense. "When Pete saw me at Gam's house, he realized I might discover what he'd done. He couldn't be sure I hadn't found the letters, so they got me thrown into jail, where Clay could learn what I knew. All the time I thought Clay was interested in me, he was just keeping watch for his grandfather."

Bobby took my hand in his. I didn't have to tell him how stupid this all made me feel—how gullible. We'd known each other so long, we could almost read each other's thoughts. "They probably figured once you got out of jail, you'd leave town as soon as possible. They didn't count on how stubborn you are."

"Yep, that's me. Good old stubborn Shandra."

Bobby sat back as a nurse appeared in the doorway. "Ready for your medicine?" she asked with a smile that showed more teeth than the average great white shark. I was ready for my pain meds in more ways than one.

Once she was gone, I pulled up my blankets and lay back on the bed. "Was it just a coincidence that they killed Harding the same day I showed up?" I asked Bobby.

"Maybe he recognized the obituary photograph just like your grandfather's partner did. Maybe he showed up at your grandmother's house a little after you. Or maybe Pete was holding him captive, trying to figure out what to do with him." Bobby ran a finger lightly across the bandages on my arm.

I could feel the medicine kicking in. Or maybe it was just my own exhaustion. My eyes began to droop. "Be a pal," I told Bobby. "Go down and get me a burger, huh? I could really use some greasy food right about now."

Bobby stood up. "Go to sleep, and I'll take you out for anything you want as soon as you get out of here."

"Hey, come on. I saved your life out there. If I hadn't fallen on Pete . . ." My mind was playing strange games with me. I couldn't seem to remember what I was going to say.

"Nice try," Bobby answered, straightening my pillow. "But I saved your life too."

"What about . . . that . . . time . . . Darth . . . Brad—"

Before I could finish reminding him about Darth, I fell asleep.

CHAPTER FIFTY-TWO

"You're sure you want to do this?" Bobby, with one freckled forearm sticking out the driver's side widow of his car, kept any hint of emotion from his voice. I knew what he meant just the same.

"I'm okay. Really. It's just . . ." I stared out the window as we bounced over the swells and potholes of the old dirt road in Bobby's boxy sedan, trying to come up with words for what I was feeling. I wasn't scared to be coming back one last time—the bad guys were in jail, and the ghosts had been laid to rest. And I wasn't under any illusions of magic the way I'd been at first.

We drove over the rise, reddish dust from the road coating the car's blue plastic upholstery, and Gam's house came into view.

Not the real one—that was gone for good.

The one I saw in my mind still had buttercups growing along the walkway where Gam and I walked. *Hold it under your chin. Your skin turned gold. That means you like butter.* The lilacs were trimmed back but bursting with a profusion of color and scent, and the porch was freshly painted. *Let's sit in the shade with a glass of cold cider, and I'll tell you about the little girl who wished she was a fairy princess.*

Bobby pulled the car to a stop, and before I could get my door open, he was around the side helping me step out as if I were some kind of invalid. He didn't follow me, though. Perched against the front bumper of his car like a watchful father, he let me walk up the grassy hillside alone.

A warm breeze soughed gently through the treetops, washing my face with the tangy bitter scent of pine and aspen. If I listened hard enough, I could almost hear it telling the story of a little boy and girl who trailed breadcrumbs into the deep dark woods. They thought they were canny enough to find their way back. But the woods can be confusing—even for grownups.

Running my fingers across the tips of the tall grass, I knew why I'd come here one last time.

"Hello, Gam." I let my words carry softly on the breeze, trusting that they'd find their intended recipient. A recipient who maybe wasn't all that far away—just out of sight. "You've been waiting for me, haven't you? Waiting for me to find the truth. You knew I wouldn't give up until I did."

Sunlight caressed the back of my head and neck with a gentle hand, and a feeling of well-being permeated my body—the same feeling I'd had as a little girl when Gam knelt at my bedside, her warm fingers curled around mine, as I feel asleep.

"I guess you wanted me to learn something from this, huh? You were always a teacher. Was it Grandpa? Did you want me to know the truth about him? Or were you trying to teach me that everyone has to endure trials in their life?" That wasn't it. There was something else I was supposed to understand.

Dozens of grasshoppers rose up from the tall stalks in front of me, leaping every which way to escape the giant invading their home. One of them landed on the back of my hand and a picture came into my head—my mother running through this same meadow, laughing with delight as clouds of tiny green insects exploded into the air in front of her.

For perhaps the first time in my life I realized that my mother had loved this place as much as I had. She'd walked the same paths, listened to the same stories—dreamed the same dreams?

"Mom?" My hand rose to my lips. The ground suddenly felt unstable beneath my feet. The trees around me doubled and then trebled. I touched my finger to my eyes, and unexpectedly they came away wet.

What was this all about? I couldn't possibly be grieving for my mother after all these years. And yet I felt as if I'd just lost her all over again—as if the car crash that took her life had been only this morning and not eighteen years before.

I pressed my hands over my mouth trying to stifle the little sobs that wanted to come out. This was crazy. I'd come to terms with my mother's loss years ago. I'd experienced the heartache, and time had healed it.

But had I come to terms?

Now that I thought about it, the emotion I remembered best was anger. Anger at my mother for leaving me. Anger at my father for deserting us. Anger at Gam for making me go on with my life. I'd spent so much time being angry that I never allowed myself time to mourn.

"Mom . . . I . . . . miss you." The words came stiffly, like a long, embedded thorn. But as soon as they were out, I realized just how true they were. I loved Gam, but I'd missed having my mother—talking to her, learning from her, knowing her. Had I been repressing those feelings through the years?

"I never really appreciated you when I was a kid. You were just there, like the sun and the moon. Then one day you weren't." The feeling of relief as I spoke was inexpressible. I'd been carrying around a huge weight all my life, and until this moment I hadn't even realized it.

"Before I came here, I never considered that you were as human as me—with desires, and dreams, and fears. I always thought of you as a picture on the wall. Something the other kids had that I didn't." From down on the lake, the burr of a speedboat engine floated on the air, and the sound of a woman's laughter.

"Dad courted you here. Were you nervous when you met him—hot and cold and achy all at the same time? Did you say awkward things when he was around?

"It must have hurt you so much when he left. I was only seven—caught up in my own pain, I didn't even think about what you must have been going through. I wish I could have been there for you—could have understood."

A warm drop slipped down my cheek. This time I didn't mind. It wasn't sorrow that made me cry, but a kinship I'd never known before. As though she'd been not only my mother, but also my sister—my friend.

This was my heritage. I might be too stubborn. My hair might never stay where it was supposed to. I might eat too much, and I might turn into a complete imbecile around guys. But I was born of solid stock. The women in my family could take the worst the world had to offer and come out standing.

I could be proud of them.

From down the road came the chug, chug, chug, of an old pickup truck. I turned in time to see it appear over the rise. It was caked with dust, and the engine wheezed like a tired pack mule. Bobby turned nervously, his hand dropping to the holster on his hip. For just a second my pulse took off like a bobsled. Then, just as quickly, it subsided.

The man behind the wheel wore a baseball cap pulled low over his eyes. His skin was lined and wrinkled from years in the sun. The tufts of unruly hair that escaped the cap were a tangled gray. But it wasn't Pete.

Pulling to a stop behind Bobby's car, he raised a gnarled hand in my direction. His lips raised, revealing a pink tongue sticking out between what few teeth he still owned. Pushing open the door, he stepped around the truck bed, which was filled with tools and odds and ends of lumber.

"'Lo, Shandra," he said, his voice soft and a little unsure.

I returned his wave and walked down to meet him.

"Hello, Trevor."

CHAPTER FIFTY-THREE

"Good to see you again." Bobby shook Trevor's hand. I could see him studying the old man's eyes and checking his breath for alcohol. He knew what I intended to do, and even though Trevor had saved my life more than once, Bobby wasn't sure he approved.

"I'm glad you came." Standing on tiptoes, I wrapped my good arm around Trevor's shoulders. For a moment he just stood there, face growing bright red from his collar to the tips of his ears. Gently—studiously avoiding my hurt ribs—he raised his arms and returned my hug. I expected him to be nothing but a bag of bones, but there was still plenty of wiry muscle in his arms and shoulders.

"I heard you came by the hospital while I was sleeping," I said.

Trevor studied his ragged fingernails. "Jus' thought I'd check on ya. Them nurses'll stick ya fulla needles and pills if ya don't keep a eye on 'em."

"Bobby says you were the one who told the sheriff where to look for me when they realized I'd been kidnapped."

"Shoulda figured it out sooner," Trevor said, kicking a dusty boot at the edge of the road. "Shoulda known Elsie'd never 'a done nothing like that. Guess I got a few wires crossed upstairs." He tapped a finger against the side of his head.

I pulled his hand away from his head, holding it in mine. "I think you're wonderful, and I'm sure Gam did too. You saved my life by getting Bobby and Sheriff Orr to the barn when you did. And you saved it before by pulling me out of the fire, didn't you?"

His cheeks red with embarrassment, Trevor slowly nodded. He rubbed the back of his hand across his eyes. "If I'd a got here little bit sooner, coulda stopped that fire altogether. Wished I coulda kept Elsie's house from burning."

We all turned toward the gutted remains of Gam's house. "You think there's any way of rebuilding it?" I asked.

"Reckon you'd have ta tear her down an' start from the ground up."

"You think you could do it?"

"Me? I ain't done nothing but jackleg fer years. You go'n get yaself one'a them contractors."

I took a deep breath, glancing briefly at Bobby. "It's just that I thought you'd want to be the one to work on your own house."

Trevor turned to look at me, eyes filled with bewilderment. "'At's not my house. I ain't got no house. Only my truck and my camp."

"Not anymore," I said, squeezing his hand. "I signed the deed over to you this morning. It's all yours."

In my hand, Trevor's fingers began to tremble. His eyes grew fuzzy. "No. That ain't . . . I can't never . . ."

"Gam would have wanted you to. I think that's part of the reason she sent me here."

Trevor continued to shake his head, his mouth moving soundlessly.

"If you need money for materials, I can probably help you get a loan," I said, noticing the way Bobby was grinning in spite of himself.

For the first time, Trevor seemed to realize that the house really was his—at least what was left of it. "I got some money from a pension and my social secu'ty." Tears were streaming down his face, but he hardly seemed to notice. "I kin fix her up jus' like new. I got my tools, an' I know where they's cheap lumber, an' . . ."

He turned and stared into my eyes, his face filled with open gratitude. "Ain't nobody ever give me nuthin' b'fore."

"It's time someone did," I said. "In fact, it's way overdue."

By the time Bobby and I left, Trevor was pacing around the remains of the house, taking measurements and jotting down notes on the back of an old envelope. He was muttering incoherently to himself and barely noticed us as we got back into the car. But that was okay. The magic was back again. I could feel it clearly.

And somewhere nearby, I thought, Gam was smiling.

CHAPTER FIFTY-FOUR

Getting back to work always takes a while. There's too much to do and not enough time to get it done. Chad, my editor, spent twenty minutes telling me how close he had come to firing me and then thought to ask how I was feeling. I didn't mind. It was good to be at work, and it was good to be home.

I wrote up the story of what happened at Echo Lake, holding out a few of the details that didn't really need telling. It was a good story, and Chad forgave my absence as soon as he read it. He asked if I wanted to go back and do an interview or two, just to fill things out. I told him no.

By the end of the day, I'd worked through most of my e-mails, finished two more stories, showed off my war wounds to my coworkers, and ate a huge dinner with Bobby at Lemon Tiger, a little Thai place we both like.

When I pulled Royce—once again running with his usual vim and vigor—into the garage, I was exhausted. My apartment was pretty much like I'd left it. No magic fairy had finished my laundry or vacuumed the carpets. But Mrs. Truxel, my landlady, had piled my mail and newspapers on the dining room table and had kept Roget and Webster, my goldfish, fed while I was gone.

I considered showering and then decided that it could wait until morning. What I really wanted was a night in my own bed, in my own pajamas, with a good book. As I changed, I noticed the music box on my dresser—the twin of Gam's, it had belonged to my mother until she died.

Picking it up, I sat on the edge of the bed. I turned it over in my hands, examining the edges. What were the odds? Surely after all these years of playing with it, I'd have noticed anything out of the ordinary. I ran my fingers lightly across the bottom corner.

And what if there actually were a compartment in this box as well. Did I want to see whatever was inside? Hadn't I discovered enough secrets for a while? I'd be better off to leave it where it was. Let the past stay in the past. Maybe at some point in the future when—

I pressed on the bottom corner and nothing happened. Gam's music box had been the only one with the secret compartment after all. It was probably for the best. My mother was entitled to keep her secrets safe. Although I have to admit I felt just a twinge of disappointment. Okay maybe more than a twinge. I guess there was still a part of me hoping to find out I was really a princess . . . or maybe I'm just a snoop.

Before returning the box to its place on the dresser, I fiddled a little more with the panel. It seemed to give beneath my touch. I jiggled the edge and it moved. Slowly, as if the springs were stripped of their strength, a secret compartment slid open.

There was something inside.

Heart pounding, I pulled out a single letter. It was addressed to my mother. There was no return address, but the postmark was Chicago, Illinois. Although the ink was blurred, I could just make out the date, March 13, 1983— about four weeks after my father had left.

With trembling fingers, I pulled open the envelope and slid out a single sheet of paper. The handwriting was bold and looked as if it had been penned in a rush.

Dear Trinny,

I know this sounds crazy, but I had to leave to protect you and the kids. Can't say anything else or tell you where I am in case someone else gets their hands on this letter. Will contact you as soon as it's safe.

Yours in love forever.

It was signed Steve Covington.
My father.